IMMORTAL THRONE

J. C. McKenzie

Harper A. Brooks

BOOKS BY J. C. MCKENZIE

Isle and Eyrie

Cormorant Run

Heir of the Eyrie

House of Moon and Stars

The Night House

House of Chaos (forthcoming)

Crawford Investigations

Conspiracy of Ravens

Nevermore

Queen of Corvids

The Call of Corvids

From the Shadows

Into the Fire

Dark Legacy

Embrace the Flame (forthcoming)

The Carus Series

Shift Happens

Beast Coast

Carpe Demon

Shift Work

Beast of All

Obsidian Flame

Dangerous Dreams

Dangerous Liaisons

Dangerous Decisions

That Old Black Magic

The Good Griffin

Standalones

Call of the Deep (The Shucker's Booktique)

Stormbound (Be My Love)

Immortal Throne (with Harper A. Brooks)

BOOKS BY HARPER A. BROOKS

Reaper Reborn

Death Wish

Death Trap

Death Match

Death Deals

Death Sentence

Till Death

Christmas Spirits: A Holiday Novella

Halfling for Hire: A Short Story Collection

Sin Demons

Playing with Hellfire

Hell in a Handbasket

All Shot to Hell

To Hell and Back

When Hell Freezes Over

Hell on Earth

Snowball's Chance in Hell: A Holiday Novella

Moon Kissed

Wolf Hunter

Wolf Tamer

Wolf Protector

Wolf Santa: A Holiday Novella

Kings of Eden

At the Mercy of Monsters

Kings of Eden

Stolen Paradise

Ruthless Lies

Shifters Unleashed

Tiger Claimed

Wolf Marked

Standalones

His Haven

Eternally Yours

Monstrous: A Monster Romance Novella

Immortal Throne

IMMORTAL THRONE

J. C. McKenzie

Harper A. Brooks

COPYRIGHT INFORMATION

Immortal Throne

Contact Information: jcmckenzie@jcmckenzie.ca

Cover Art: Natasha Art

Publishing History:

First JCM Publications Edition, 2022

ISBN: 978-1-990143-11-3 (ebook)

ISBN: 978-1-990143-10-6 (print)

THIS BOOK CONTAINS
EXPLICIT LANGUAGE,
SEX SCENES, THE
ENEMIES TO LOVERS
TROPE, AND ELEMENTS
OF DEATH, GRIEF,
MURDER, AND FORCED
PROXIMITY. IT IS
INTENDED FOR
MATURE READERS.

To Bennett,
My brave little boy

— HARPER A. BROOKS

To Dad,
I hope you never read this one

— J. C. MCKENZIE

CHAPTER ONE

T he bell rang.

It was such a simple sound, but one that automatically got my blood pumping and my mind racing. The need to win, fight, scrape, and claw surged through me in an instant. The flashing lights, snarling crowd, and smell of sweat and blood around me faded into the background. There was nothing but me, my opponent, and the thundering of my heartbeat as my adrenaline kicked up a few notches.

I stared at the man in front of me. Short, but thick at the arms and neck, his muscles glistened with sweat from the oppressive heat of the Underground, a secret fighting arena where people like me came to bet money or fight for the prize.

One thing was for sure—whether spectating or fighting, everyone in the Underground had their demons and they were all here to forget them or leave them behind.

Me?

I was here to beat the shit out of them.

"It's a shame we have to fight, Sloane." My opponent held his hands up, and unfurling his fingers, waved at me to come get him. His Irish accent was thick, and he was all smiles. Cocky. Like most new to the Underground. "I planned to ask you out for a pint."

Not the worst pick-up line I've heard, but not the best either.

"Yeah, I'll just have to embarrass you instead." I hopped from foot to foot, my body limber and ready from my pre-match warm-up. The air was muggy in the crowded space, making it harder to breathe, but it was something I'd become accustomed to from my frequent trips here. My shorts, tight and hugging my butt, let me move freely while my sports bra kept the girls firmly in place. Those not involved or knowledgeable about mixed martial arts, or MMA, might think I wore the revealing sports gear to show off my body. In reality, I wore this outfit to stay cool, move without restriction, and make it difficult for my opponent to hold me with my clothing or use it to choke me out.

The man swung one of his meaty fists, but I dodged with a quick v-step. He came at me with the left next, and I ducked before striking him in the ribs. My hit surprised him. By the wince on his face, I'd say the strength I had behind it caught him off guard, too.

That was one of my advantages. I might be skinnier than most of the muscleheads frequenting this joint, but I knew how to fight. And thanks to years of jujitsu, kickboxing, and living on the poorer streets of Braton, I was pretty good at it, too.

I also had a little secret talent not many knew about. My sixth sense, or hindsight as I liked to call it. It was a small paranormal gift I'd acquired from my father—whoever the fuck he was—because my mother was as human as they came. If danger approached, I sensed and usually avoided it, giving me even more of an upper hand in the Underground.

So, when my opponent decided to try something sly and reached for my ponytail, my internal alarms went off. The familiar tingling warned me just in time to swivel out of his way, spin, and elbow him right in the mouth. He reeled back, holding his split lip, and cursed. The crowd around the tall cage erupted with cheers, drowning out his shouts, and I grinned.

He was making this almost too easy.

As long as I didn't pass out again, this fight was going to be a cake-walk.

I'd been coming here for years. Ever since I was eighteen and able to, according to the rules. That was pretty much the only rule in this place.

As expected, I lost a lot in the beginning. My crooked nose and scar above my right eye proved it. But now, I'd made a name for myself. *Now*, when I stepped into the cage, people knew not to bet against me.

I rarely lost.

As the Irishman charged me, I crouched and swiped out with my leg, catching him behind the knee. He hit the floor like a ton of bricks. After a second or two, he visibly shook himself and grabbed for my ankles. With excitement spiking, I danced away from his grubby hands. When he stood again, fury blazed in his eyes.

Didn't like getting his ass handed to him by a woman, huh? Most of these pig-headed male fighters were the same. He'd learn soon enough. In addition to my hindsight, I had additional strength, too.

I held up my bruised and taped-up fists again as the Irishman glared.

As I waited for him to come at me again, my vision blurred.

Oh no.

Not again.

My opponent's tense shoulders, bloody face, and hate-filled expression became nothing more than a fuzzy outline of shapes and color. Heat prickled across my skin. The hair on the back of my neck rose.

I'm going to go down. Again.

This wasn't my hindsight; there was nothing paranormal about it. I needed to return Dr. Callahan's call about these random fainting spells. He said he had the test results. Maybe I needed to drink more water. Maybe I had some sort of vitamin D deficiency or a lingering concussion. I didn't know. I wasn't a doctor.

Or it could be something more. Something...deadlier.

Like cancer. Like she had.

A sense of foreboding swept over me, my internal warning system blaring full alert. At the same time, images of a heart-wrenching past crashed down around me. My mother's face floated to the surface, her cheeks sunken in, purple darkening the skin around her eyes. No longer the hardass woman who'd never hesitated to speak her mind—she became a shell of herself at the end. Barely the person who'd raised me off two minimum wage jobs and rice and beans for dinner. I'd never known someone as hardworking and determined as her, and when I had to hold her hand that final time in the hospital, I couldn't believe she was gone.

Devastated didn't come close to describing my emotional state.

It had always been me and her against the world. And now, I was alone. Truly alone.

I wobbled on my feet, my head light despite my heavy thoughts.

And that was when I got sucker-punched in the face and the lights went out for good.

I WOKE UP TO THE ROAR OF THE CROWD, THIS TIME cursing and spitting at me. With my face plastered to the rough canvas, violent and intense pain radiated across my cheek and jaw.

Oh, fuck, it hurt. I hadn't been hit like this since...I don't know when. But I didn't miss it.

I pushed off the cage's floor and stood. My vision spun and I stumbled to the side. My head hurt just as much from the impact with the ground as it did from the Irishman's fist. The Underground didn't use the high quality mats official fighting organizations do. This shit was rock hard, cracked, and covered in stains from god-knows-what.

I rubbed the side of my face to ease the sharpness but pulled away when new pain shot through my head. My fingers came back bloody.

Great. More scars.

My body was littered with them. My arms, legs, and back didn't bother me too much, but my face? Those were harder to hide or explain away, and I wasn't exactly trained in the fine art of makeup application.

I blinked, trying to refocus, and found Greg, the Underground's main bookie. He made his rounds through the stands, collecting money from some very pissed-off audience members.

"Come on, come on! Fork it over!" he called as he practically ripped a wad of money out of a man's hand.

"She threw the match," he barked back. "It's rigged."

"What kind of establishment do you think I'm

fucking running here? You bet wrong. Time to pay." But when Greg hopped down the bleachers, he caught my gaze and a sympathetic smile tugged on his lips.

Of course, he knew I didn't throw anything. He'd seen enough of these fights to know I should've won.

And I should have. It was why I bet heavily on myself every match.

Now I had nothing.

I'd bet a lot on this match, too much, knowing the odds were in my favor.

In hindsight, totally stupid, but I had bills to pay.

Still woozy, I gripped the ring's metal gate to help me stand. The coolness helped ground my spinning head. On the other side, the Irishman was celebrating by pounding his chest and shouting, like a hairless ape. *Charming.*

I moved toward the exit, my feet heavy as if made from lead. The flashing lights threatened to blind me, the cheers, screams and curses from the crowd thundered in my ears. My pride stung more than my face, and I just wanted to get out of here before the angry crowd followed me.

"Oi! Girlie!"

I turned to find the macho Irishman stalking over to me. Arms swinging by his side, and muscled legs moving stiffly, he looked like he couldn't quite walk properly with all the testosterone flowing through his veins.

He was the last person I wanted to deal with right now. "Girlie? I'm twenty-five fucking years old."

His eyes widened. Either he didn't expect my age, or he didn't expect my fresh mouth, but either way, surprise, shithead. I walked down the steps toward the pits to where the fighters changed and whatnot before and after matches.

"Wait!" he yelled.

I stopped again to look at him with a raised eyebrow. "You won. Can you just leave it alone?"

"Throw some ice on that pretty face and meet me at the bar in a half-hour," he said, his smart-ass grin back in place.

"You're joking, right?"

"I'll even pay."

"You can fuck right off." Without sparing him another look, I trudged off and headed for the pits to gather my stuff and get out of this hellhole. Now, I needed to find another way to earn the money I'd lost tonight. And I had no idea how I was going to do it.

My savings were gone. I had enough for this month's rent and enough credit to see me through the next month, but the rest?

Nothing.

Stupid, stupid, stupid.

Times like this made me wish I had taken the path Mom wanted for me. As much as she'd hoped I'd do better than her and find a steady 401k job, I couldn't sit behind a desk. Working a nine-to-five was Hell on

Earth in my book and not my thing. So, I got my money by doing more unconventional things.

I winced as the next step sent jarring pain racing up my back to the base of my skull along with memories of some of my more unconventional jobs. I'd even worked as a phone sex operator but got too creeped out and quit after two weeks.

Fighting was the only thing that stuck for me. And when the payout was good, I could go weeks between matches.

It was a win-win for me.

Well, until tonight.

Now the dizzy spells threatened to take my livelihood from me. I'd never had a fainting spell during a fight before, but with it happening more and more, how was I supposed to fight? And no fights meant no money.

After changing my clothes and cleaning the grime and blood from my face under the flickering dull lights, I emerged out of the Underground's secret entrance. Not many people knew about the fight club hidden in the basement of the abandoned bottle factory, but that was the point. It hadn't stayed under law enforcement's radar this long by accident, after all.

Hiking my duffle bag higher onto my shoulder, I walked down the dark and smelly alleyway toward the road. Even at night, the air, still sticky and warm from the hot summer's day, clung to my skin. My tank stuck to my torso and my track pants made my legs feel like they were in some sort of sauna torture device.

The sudden tickle of my hindsight made me pause. I scanned the shadows, but nothing leapt out at me. The roar of an engine coming to life made me jump, and the flare of a headlight faded away as a motorcycle passed.

Not completely odd, since we lived in a city, it was a humid night, and the Underground was filled with all kinds of people. So then, why did the biker make my Spidey senses tingle?

My gaze swept the alley again. Two of the Underground's security guards smoked near the entrance, but they were too occupied in their conversation to bother with me. Otherwise, the alley was empty.

Hmm... Maybe whatever was going on with my health affected my sixth sense, too. Wouldn't surprise me. I seemed to have the worst luck in the world.

With a deep sigh, I continued walking. An ice bath and some ibuprofen called my name.

I can't believe I lost.

CHAPTER TWO

My thighs stuck to the plastic chair in the small room as the older doctor sitting across from me continued to speak, spilling all sorts of medical information. The words washed over me. After he said terminal organ failure, really, what else was there to say?

I came to Dr. Callahan about the fainting spells and expected something simple like the need to drink more water or pop a multivitamin but, as it turned out, I was dying.

The clock's second hand kept moving—tick, tick, tick. The computer on the desk behind the doctor kept humming. The people in the waiting room outside kept talking, the low murmur of their voices traveling through the seams around the closed door.

Life kept moving even though mine was falling down all around me.

What was I going to do with Chupey?

Maybe Becca would take care of him.

No, that wouldn't work. She hated dogs.

I wish Mom was here.

The cool air-conditioning brushed over my bare arms. I shivered and regretted choosing another tank top for today's appointment.

I...I didn't want to die. I was only twenty-five. There were so many things I wanted to do, places I wanted to go, book boyfriends I wanted to have fictional relationships with, and television couples to ship.

I'd only felt a little tired. That was it. A few fainting spells were the only sign something was wrong. I'd thought my iron levels were low and suspected I might be anemic or something to do with fighting in the cage. Not this. Not *dying*.

I wasn't prepared for this, even after all the poking and prodding over the last few weeks.

I forced my hands to relax and took a deep, calming breath.

Of course, it didn't fucking work.

The doctor looked at me expectantly, blinking and waiting.

"I'm sorry, what did you say?" I asked, clutching my backpack in my lap. Maybe he was wrong. Maybe they were all wrong and this was just some sick joke.

Dr. Callahan flashed me a small, sad smile before speaking. "I've already called over to BCH. There's a bed waiting for you, and I've already called their team of specialists and briefed them on your case. We just need you to sign some forms to get started."

BCH? I barely heard anything beyond that. Braton Community Hospital was where my mother spent her last days. And died.

I couldn't go there.

He must've read my answer from my expression because he quickly followed up with, "I want to help you. We may not know what this is now, but maybe if we monitor you more closely, get a few more tests—"

"No." The word snapped from my lips so harshly, Dr. Callahan stepped back. Panic started to claw at my insides just at the thought of being stuck in a hospital bed, forced to live out my remaining hours staring at the white walls and hearing the monitors around me beep. I didn't want that to be my reality. "No, no. I can't."

The doctor cleared his throat. "The mystery of this ailment means there's no cure, but it also means there's still hope."

Ha! Right. I'd had a lot of hope when Mom first got her cancer diagnosis. That hadn't turned out well for either of us, since she was currently in the fucking ground.

Dr. Callahan studied me, his dark brown gaze warm and sympathetic. The skin around his eyes and mouth had the telltale wrinkles of someone who smiled and laughed a lot. He certainly wasn't doing any of that now.

"Sloane, please. This may be the only way we can fix this."

"Thank you, doctor," I said dismissively and pushed out of the chair. The skin stuck to the plastic made a loud sound like wet Velcro as it released its hold on the chair. Wincing, I brushed the wrinkles from my khaki shorts and quickly went for the door. *Get me out of here.* "I appreciate your help."

"Take a few days to think about it," he called out. "If you change your mind, you have my number."

I hurried out of the doctor's examination room, both numb and vibrating with anxiety, like I wasn't part of this reality anymore. The waiting area was a blur of faces and empty chairs, yet it took forever to cross the room to the doors outside. When I finally stepped out of the air-conditioned office, the heat smacked me in the face. The humidity clung to me as I took a deep breath of thick summer air.

The sound of traffic and construction rumbled down the street along with the constant buzz of insects. Across the road, a statue of some general stood at the town center with a plaque I'd never cared to read, and BCH was on the other side, next to the train station.

My stomach sank like it did every time I saw that place and automatically searched for the corner room on the third floor. The room where Mom died a year ago.

More memories flooded back and, like the last time I stood in the cage, they immobilized me. Mom's sunken face. The sympathetic nurses. The horns of the train blaring while I held Mom's hand and watched her take her last breath.

I swallowed, my mouth dry. I'd hear those horns again, but this time it would be me dying, me withering away in a hospital bed with over-starched sheets and an overworked, under-appreciated nurse trying their best to stay positive. But I wouldn't have a family member by my side.

Maybe Becca would come, but my friend had been distant lately. Without her, I had no friends. At least no human friends. I couldn't bring my dog to the hospital. If Becca didn't visit, there'd be no one to hold my hand except maybe the nurse. I might very well have to do this alone and that scared me the most.

"God, that's an ugly dog." A man in his twenties strolled down the sidewalk holding the hand of a beautiful woman. He sneered down at a dog resting in the shade with its leash tied to a tree.

Right where I'd left him.

Under other circumstances, I might've considered the tall, fit man attractive. But he'd just insulted my dog and now I wanted to punch him in the throat.

Chupey was part Xoloitzcuintle, part mutt and part three-year-old toddler with attachment issues. Lean and well-muscled, he had a wedge-shaped face, constantly wrinkled brow, yellow eyes, and large pointed ears that swiveled around like satellite dishes.

My dog didn't exactly have the kind of doggy good looks that made random strangers fawn over him. Instead, Chupey liked to eat raw hotdogs and fart and had no concept of personal space. But he was mine, and I loved him. He shared my general distrust for strangers, biting first and asking questions later. He'd been at my side for the last ten years, and after Mom died, he'd been my only true companion besides Becca.

My stomach twisted. Who would take care of him after I was gone?

The woman holding the jerk's hand giggled, hiding her bright white teeth with her hand. "I think he's cute. Ugly-cute, you know? I think he's one of those Mexican hairless dogs."

Though Chupey was mostly hairless, he had a tuft of fur on the top of his head that looked like a mohawk. Really, how much more badass could he get? He looked like the lovechild of a hyena and a Chupacabra, the infamous demonic creature of myths and legends.

The man turned to his girlfriend, eyes wide. "That dog has a face only a mother could love."

I'd heard enough. That was my ugly dog baby they were talking about.

"Hey!" I called out, startling them both. Normally, I would've ignored all the things and let their mean remarks go. But, unfortunately for them, today wasn't a normal day. "His mom's right here and unlike him, I woke up this morning and chose violence."

They glanced at each other and quickly walked by me, not making eye contact.

That's right, keep moving. After the news I just got, I was done being nice and considerate of other peoples' feelings.

Chupey watched the whole thing, wagging his long, whip-like tail.

"I suppose you think all this is hilarious?" I untied the leash and held the loop in my hand.

He looked up at me and barked as if to say yes.

"Of course, you do." He probably thought it was also hilarious that I lost all my money betting on myself and needed to find a way to make some of it back, and fast. Maybe I should stay home. Just this once. Eat a gallon of ice cream in my fuzzy PJs with *The Price is Right* on loop.

I turned toward my apartment on 70th street and headed down the sidewalk. The heat coming off the pavement caressed my calves as if Hell itself planned to open up the road and swallow me whole.

Not yet. I had some living left to do.

CHAPTER THREE

"You're late," Becca said, not even looking up from her drink as she gulped it down. "Like, later than what's typically late for you."

With an hourglass figure squeezed into a form-fitting dress, flawless skin, ash-blonde hair and expressive blue eyes, Becca could've been a pin-up model, porn star, or hell, whatever she wanted to be. And what did she choose as her profession?

Heartbreaker.

And men paid her for the honor.

Still out of breath, I fumbled to hang the strap of my bag on the back of the chair. When I sat down, my knees bumped the table, rattling the silverware and knocking over the salt. I ran my sweaty palms over my denim shorts and offered my friend an apologetic smile.

Without missing a beat, Becca picked up the

shaker, poured some salt into her hand, and tossed it over her left shoulder, before setting it upright on the table. Any other day, I'd tease her for her beliefs in ridiculous superstitions, but since she was already pissed at me for leaving her hanging, I kept it to myself.

"I'm sorry—"

She held up a hand to stop me. "I don't want to hear it, Sloane. I really don't. I've known you for what? Five years now? And every birthday dinner, every midday meet-up, every nightclub outing, it doesn't matter. You're always late. I've come to expect it now."

"Then why do you sound so annoyed with me?" I asked. My back stiffened and my skin prickled. I didn't need the guilt trip.

Did I deserve it? Absolutely.

But did Becca need to lay into me right now? No.

"You should know by now that this is just who I am as a human being," I said. "For what it's worth, I am sorry. I hadn't meant to be this late. I got tied up on an important phone call." Which was true. I had. One that involved finding Chupey a possible new home for when I was gone. Just thinking about how quickly my life had spiraled and had turned into an all out dumpster fire stabbed at my heart.

She scoffed and started collecting her sunglasses and purse, about to leave. "I wish I could be as inconsiderate and selfish as you and not care that I left my friend sitting here for forty-five minutes. I have things to do, Sloane. I have places to be. I can't just sit around here all day waiting for your irresponsible ass to show up. It's rude and—"

"I'm dying."

The words fell from my mouth. Part of me wished I hadn't blurted the news. At least not like this. But the other part was relieved to have the truth out. When Becca went off on me, she could go on forever, and how else was I going to explain my extraordinary lateness today? Everything else she'd see as an excuse.

She blinked rapidly. Confused, of course. I did just drop a bomb on her.

"Wait...*what*?"

Sitting still and forcing my shoulders and arms to remain relaxed, I tried to appear cool as a cucumber, but my hands shook. "I'm dying."

She plopped her stuff back on the table and leaned forward. "You're fucking with me," she whispered.

"I wish I was." I sighed heavily. "Remember me telling you about my random fainting spells. Well, I went to the doctor yesterday to talk about my test results..."

Her gaze searched my face for a long time, waiting for the "ah, gotcha" moment, but when she saw it wasn't coming, she paled. "Wait a minute. What's going on? You wouldn't lie about—not something like this."

"I'm not lying." I never lied. Sure, I wasn't perfect. I had faults, but lying wasn't one of them.

She shook her head, refusing to believe it. "No way. You can't be... You can't be dying. What did the doctor say exactly? Cancer like your mom? That stuff can run in families, right? There are cures, treatments—"

"Not cancer. They don't know what it is, but my body is shutting down. If things continue shutting down at this rate, I don't have a lot of time left. My doctor thinks I only have a month or two..."

"A month or two!"

Other restaurant patrons turned our way, and I hushed her sharply. "Is there an echo in here? Yes, that's what I said—what *he* said, I mean."

"I-I don't believe it. I don't."

"Well, believe it or not, it's true. The doctor prescribed me a handful of pills to swallow every day, but so far they do nothing but make me lose sleep and want to throw up. I can barely focus on anything too long, and I'm worried when I fight—"

"Don't tell me you're still going to the Underground," she snapped, cutting me off mid-sentence.

Clamping my mouth shut, I realized my mistake. Like Mom, Becca never liked my *unusual* hobby. I took her with me once to sit in the crowd and watch me, and she had to leave before the first round. Didn't even see me take a swing. It was too grimy and brutal for her. Or so she said.

She hadn't shut up about my fighting since then.

When I didn't answer her, she seized her opportunity to ream me out. "You're telling me you are still fighting in a cage, like a wild animal, for scraps?"

"Scraps? We don't fight for food. I'm not in the circus or something. It's for money. And a lot of it, too. It's how I'm able to pay my bills. I'm good at it." Or, at least I was. I hadn't gone back since my loss and diagnosis.

I thought back to my fight with the Irishman a few days ago, and how the dizziness had come over me with no warning, leaving me disoriented and stumbling.

I still had the gnarly gash on my cheek as my parting gift.

Without realizing it, I swiped my hair behind my ear, and Becca's gaze narrowed on the spot I was just thinking about.

"Jesus, Sloane. Does that hurt?" she asked and reached out to me. I jerked back. "It looks like it hurts."

"It stings a little, but nothing to cry over." I waved her hand away. As always, I appreciated her concern for me, as annoying as it was sometimes. When things got bad for me, like when I lost Mom, Becca was there for me. Even when I thought I didn't want her to be. And friends like that were hard to come by.

She cared. She just had a strange way of showing it sometimes, but I did, too.

"Did you lose?" she asked.

I winced. I don't know why, but that hurt more than the cut on my face. Maybe because I rarely lost. My pride was wounded enough.

"Yeah. I lost," I said.

She sucked in a sharp breath. She knew better than anyone how competitive I was.

"Don't beat yourself up about it, okay? You're... going through a lot," she said.

I picked up a fork and twirled it in my hand. The server hadn't come by to take my order, but I didn't feel like eating anyway.

Becca was right, of course. I had been through a lot, and the sting of defeat lingered like it mattered. Like I wouldn't be dead soon enough.

Dropping the fork back on the table, I sighed heavily. Maybe if I didn't think about death, I could avoid the whole thing.

A chill ran through my body.

Yeah, because Mom outran it, didn't she?

I rubbed my hands over my face and leaned onto the table. Exhausted. I was completely drained. I had barely done anything all day, besides sleep in, feel sorry for myself, and make some calls. I could sleep for another ten hours straight.

Did Mom think like this when she'd gotten her diagnosis? Did she want to ignore it or just sleep the truth away? If she did, she'd kept all her fears from me. She'd been so convinced she'd beat it with treatment, just another example of what a complete badass Mom was.

And now where was she? In a plot down in St. Peter's Cemetery.

Tears sprung to my eyes, but I squeezed them shut to keep them at bay. None of this was fair. I had so little to start with and I'd lost so much already. If God was real, he must be pissing himself laughing somewhere at my expense.

What did I do to deserve such a shitty life?

A gentle hand pressed on my shoulder, but I didn't look up. I didn't need to. I knew Becca was trying her best to comfort me.

If this was any other time, I'd shove her touch away, but honestly, I just didn't have the strength to. I welcomed the warmth of her touch, the bit of empathy it brought. She was truly all I had left. Her and Chupey.

Even when she bent down and wrapped her arms around me for a hug from behind, I didn't move. She shook against me and I heard her sniffling as she tried to resist crying, too.

We stayed like that for a while. I'm not sure how long, but by the time Becca let me go and wiped her cheeks dry, my chest was tight from resisting the urge to sob uncontrollably.

"Hey," she began, voice shaky from crying, "I just took a temp job at a company in the heart of the city. Some big wig. You know how it is. Secretary work. Since you lost your fight and if you're looking for some money..."

A smile tugged at my lips. It wasn't the first time she'd offered me her position at the temp agency she worked for. Whenever I was low on cash, she'd try passing jobs along, all the types of positions that would've made Mom proud. But I was never the sit-at-a-desk type. I usually turned her offers away, unless I was truly desperate. Like now...

"It'd be a good way to keep you distracted," she went on. "Keep your mind off *things*."

I gave her a deadpan look. Becca normally didn't put this much effort trying to convince me to take her temp postings.

"Keep you out of the Underground."

"Ah, there it is. The real reason." I chuckled. I might've loved cage fighting, I might've thrived on the vicious, bloodthirsty crowd, but even I had to admit fighting might not be the best option for me if I continued to have these fainting spells.

She reached into her bag, pulled out a folded piece of paper, and handed it to me. "Here's all the info. It's good pay. Look at it. Go on."

Plucking the paper from her, I unfolded it. The numbers glared back at me, and I almost choked on my own saliva. "Does that say fifty-five dollars?"

She nodded. "An hour. Yeah. Exactly. It's a good gig and easy work. Just tend to the big bossman's requests, do a lunch run, hold his calls, reschedule meetings—you know, the stupid stuff."

"Pretty sure none of it is stupid. Assistants work their butts off."

Becca scowled. "Do you want the job or not?"

Did I really want to be some yes-man for a guy who probably earned his fortune because dear ol' daddy had a yacht—or two—and didn't know the meaning of the word no?

Absolutely not.

But did I need the money to live whatever was left of my life the way I wanted to?

"Shit, fine." I refolded the paper and stuck it into my jean pocket.

"Good girl," Becca teased.

"And what are you going to do then?" I asked her. "Don't you need the money, too?"

"Eh, not really. At least not now."

Knowing Becca, that only meant one thing. "Who's the guy?"

She blinked, pretending to be shocked by my accusation. "I don't know what you mean."

Whenever Becca didn't need to work, it was guaranteed she had a new boyfriend. Some sugar daddy who gave her anything she wanted. Money. Jewelry. Clothes. Hell, one guy even bought her a new car "just because." Who did that?

I'd certainly never been in a relationship with that kind of dynamic. But, unlike me, Becca had charisma. She had confidence, knew how to sweet talk her way to get what she wanted, and had a figure that men drooled over, and most women would kill for. Getting a boyfriend was easy for her.

Keeping them... Well, that was another story.

"Who's the new sucker you have fawning all over you now?"

She waved her hand in the air like it didn't matter who it was, as long as she got what she wanted. "Some guy I met at a coffee shop. He saw me ordering and came up to talk to me."

I rolled my eyes. "You are the only person in this world who can get a date just by looking at a menu."

"You could take a few pointers from me," Becca added. She lifted a single brow for effect. "When was the last time you went out on a date?"

"Bec, I'm dying. I don't have time to focus on my love life right now."

"Oh, yeah. Jeez. I'm sorry, girl. I wasn't thinking," Becca said.

I shook my head and said, "It doesn't matter. Thanks for listening, at least."

"Always. What are friends for?"

"Taking care of Chupey when I'm gone?"

She paled.

I laughed and waved my hand in the air. "Don't worry. I wouldn't ask that of you. I've been researching no-kill rescues and foster programs. That's actually why I was late today. I was on the phone with one for Chupey."

She eased into her seat. "Oh, well…"

I leveled her with a look.

"Thank God. I'm sorry, Sloane, but I just…"

"Hate dogs?"

She shuddered and nodded. "Ever since I got attacked by a chihuahua, I can't bring myself to go near them."

We sat for a long while, just talking, and the server eventually came by to take our orders. I settled on a mimosa. It was after five o'clock somewhere. While I drank and Becca picked at her salad, I told her more about my diagnosis. She tried to offer me words of wisdom about keeping my head up and bringing good things into my life with a positive mindset. Too bad those things never worked for me.

I highly doubted they'd save me now.

Becca wrapped her arms around me as we stood outside the restaurant saying our goodbyes.

"Thanks for showing up today," she murmured against my ear. "It was really good to see you."

"I wasn't good company," I admitted.

"You are always good company." She narrowed her eyes. "When you're on time."

There it was, the last little dig she had to get in. I squeezed her a bit tighter before leaning back.

"Please take care of yourself. And take that job. I'm serious, Sloane. You take that job and don't worry about me," Becca added.

"I already said I would take it." I tugged my shirt back in place.

Now I sounded petulant on top of everything.

Becca set me with a look before heading off down the street, her hips swinging like a pendulum as she walked. I stepped farther toward the curb, lifting my hand to hail a cab. The roar of a motorcycle ripped through the low hum of the street noise.

I jerked around, staring toward the corner where a trail of smoke rose. The motorcycle's rear wheels spun uselessly on the asphalt before it caught traction and bolted forward. I narrowed my eyes as it disappeared around the corner. Not sure why it seemed like a message for me, but the sight sent a ping of warning through my body and my hindsight tingled.

That couldn't be good.

CHAPTER FOUR

I tugged my white blouse down, straightening the creases, and stood in front of the overly wide and shiny receptionist desk. The makeup caked on my face to hide the fading bruises and the cut on my cheek suffocated my skin. After all these years of fighting, my makeup application hadn't improved. Didn't help that I'd rather be drenched in sweat trying to choke some bitch out than putting on foundation and working a "real" job.

"Sloane Davis, from the temp agency." The agency had told me to go to the top floor of this building and check in.

The blonde woman behind the counter with a tight bun and perfectly painted face glanced up from the computer screen, her expression blank and emotionless. "Mr. Dante will see you now. Go straight through."

I nodded and walked past the desk to a large set of double doors. My hindsight prickled over my skin, warning me of danger. With my hand resting on the metal handle, I hesitated. I usually listened to my instincts, but this was a bona fide posting from the temp agency. How bad could it be?

I glanced over at the front desk and the receptionist bobbed her head.

Well, now or never. I needed this job—well, at least I used to need it. Now, I wasn't so sure. What I really wanted to do was travel to Europe. Or sit on an island beach somewhere in the Caribbean. Have a few one-night stands with some questionable characters...

But even with death breathing down my neck, that still wasn't me. It wasn't who I was. Or who I wanted to be. Besides, if I had any hope of carrying out even one thing on my bucket list, I needed a healthier bank account. Losing that fight had really set me back.

Everything from my recent doctor visit came hurtling back to the surface—all the fear, anger, and uncertainty I had suppressed since the diagnosis. The emotions smacked me upside the head harder than any blow the Irishman could've thrown at me.

I staggered to the side and struggled to catch my breath. My hindsight rang incessantly in my head now.

Yeah, I got it. Dying.

I clenched my teeth together and hissed. No. Just... no. I refused to let this happen. I refused to be weak.

Instead of crumbling to the floor and sobbing like I

really wanted to, I pulled the door open and let the cool air wash over me before stepping into the large office.

A man in a suit twirled a pen in his hand. His back facing the door, he stood stiffly and looked out the floor-to-ceiling windows. When the door snicked shut behind me, he turned around.

My stomach dropped.

Tall, with broad shoulders, his sheer size was intimidating enough, but it was his breathtaking beauty making me gasp for air. Black hair as dark as a starless night sky framed his chiseled face in soft waves. Smooth, tanned skin, sharp cheekbones and a straight nose made him look like a statue.

Or a vengeful god.

He made me want to do all sorts of things without even thinking. I'd have to reconsider that whole "out of my comfort zone, one-night stands" thing.

Or, if I was lucky, then the "sleeping with my boss" thing too.

"My name is Sloane." I licked my lips and somehow managed to find my voice, even if it did come out a little more breathy than usual. "I'm the temp."

He didn't respond right away, probably put off by how I ogled him like a three-tier chocolate cake. His jacket hung open, revealing a crisp white shirt pressed flat over what had to be chiseled abs.

My heartbeat picked up a little faster. I'd never

wanted to jump someone's bones so fast in my life. This was new for me.

"I expected someone else." When he finally spoke, his deep voice sounded like rough sex in a club bathroom stall. Or, at least, that's how I'd imagine it would sound like.

"Becca was unable to take the job, so they sent me instead." I finally met his emerald-green gaze and sucked in a breath.

This wasn't a man who just laid eyes on the hired help for the first time. This wasn't a look of surprise or welcome. Or even disappointment.

Nope. Not my luck. Pure, unfettered hatred stared back at me.

Icy fear clamped onto my spine and froze me in place. The sense of impending doom from earlier returned, and my hindsight tingled to the point of shaking my limbs.

He clutched the pen in his hand so hard it snapped under the pressure. His loathing, even from this distance, was palpable. It lay heavy in the air. He might've met me today, but one thing was very clear.

He hated me.

"What...how will I be assisting you today?" I asked.

The rage quickly slipped away from his expression, as if it had never been there at all, replaced with a quirk of his full lips. "You will be my slave for the day."

Surely, I heard him wrong. "Excuse me?"

"You will be my personal assistant. I will need you

to run errands, order catering, and fetch meals at the appropriate time." He waved his hand in the air. "Will that be a problem?"

I forced a smile across my face—my customer service smile that hid how I felt inside. Irritation gnawed at my belly. None of the things he listed were beyond the scope of a personal assistant role, but I couldn't shake how he initially introduced the job, or how it seemed to amuse him.

"Of course," I said. "What line of work are you in?"

His green eyes sparked. "Transportation."

I glanced around the opulent office again. Transportation sure seemed like a great business to get into.

"But you needn't worry about the business stuff. You're here to take care of my *personal* needs."

Goosebumps rose. How did he make that sound so lecherous? "Where would you like me to start?"

"My shoes," he said.

I raised an eyebrow.

He chucked the remains of the pen on the desk, pulled out the chair and walked it around to place it a few feet away from me. Taking a seat, he slouched in the chair a little, his legs out in a total man-spread, and tapped his expensive snakeskin shoes. "They need cleaning."

I stared at them, confused as hell and a bit disgusted. Those shoes probably just came out of a box and did not need buffing or cleaning at all. What was this guy's deal?

"Sure. Do you have cleaning supplies?" I asked to cover my confusion.

He leveled me with a look. "I suggest you figure it out."

"Then I suggest you supply me with funds to carry out your wishes." Okay, so I needed to work on my social skills. This wasn't a good start, already clashing with the client. My talents leaned more toward placing my fists in people's faces. Not nodding and smiling like some people-pleasing robot.

Was he going to fire me? Part of me hoped so because my pride would never allow me to quit.

He snarled but shifted to pull out a billfold from the inside pocket of his jacket. "Cleaning supplies and coffee."

"How do you take it?"

The air vibrated with his barely contained anger, so intense, it brushed against my skin. Well, that didn't take long to re-emerge. What on Earth was so offensive about asking how he liked his coffee?

Mr. Dante flicked through a number of bills and held out a wad of cash. "Black."

Of course, that's how he took his coffee. Made perfect sense. I snatched the cash from his outstretched hand and mentally cursed my life choices. My lack of stability and love for fighting had led me down this road of temporary employment. The goal had always been to land something more "respectable" and perma-nent, make Mom proud and have a sense of normalcy and stability in my life, but employers all seemed to require degrees now for entry-level positions. They also frowned at black eyes and split lips, and I couldn't bring myself to give up the cage.

And now...what was the point? Did my past goals even matter anymore?

Mr. Dante raised his dark eyebrows. Had I stared at him this entire time?

His gaze glittered with amusement, but the rage was still there, lurking behind those green gems.

I forced another fake smile across my face and stuffed the money in my pocket. Would acting as this guy's personal slave for the day be that bad? He paid well and I needed the money. "I'll be back soon."

I turned and walked out of the room with a pocketful of hundreds. I could keep walking. He gave me enough that this would cover my salary for the day. More than the day.

I jabbed the elevator button with my pointer finger and took a deep breath. I might not be the most eligible person to employ; I lacked a lot of training and job experience thanks to getting shuffled around all the time by Mom and then my obsession with the Underground, but I had integrity. I'd see this job out.

ON MY KNEES BETWEEN MY NEW BOSS'S LEGS WAS not where I saw this day going when I got up this morning. I scrubbed the snakeskin of his expensive footwear, gently using the products the shoe guy sold me. As I expected, the shoes didn't have a spec of dirt on them. Even the soles lacked scuffing, almost as if *Mr. fucking Dante* purchased his entire outfit just for the day. His closet must be huge.

"You missed a spot." His gruff voice made me look up.

He stared down at me between his legs, contempt twisting his full lips. He'd removed his jacket and tie and unfastened the top two buttons on his white shirt while I was out. The tanned skin underneath did weird things to my heartbeat.

Maintaining eye contact, I lifted his shoe, still on his foot like he insisted, and ran the cloth along the instep. I hadn't missed a spot. And right now, I kept myself mentally stimulated by imagining all the ways I could break his face.

"That's enough," he said, shifting position. His movement pulled the material of his shirt and revealed an angry red scar on his chest. As if someone had taken a hot poker to him on the weekend, the scar looked like a fresh brand. "I need to make a call."

"Would you like me to step out?" *Please say yes.*

"No, I'd like you to hold my coffee."

I packed up the shoe-cleaning supplies and shuffled back to stand up.

He shook his head, and I froze. What did he want? Why did his lips turn up at the corner like that?

"I need somewhere to place it." He waved at the ground in front of him.

I leaned to the side to peer around him at the perfectly functional executive desk behind him.

His lips quirked and he leaned forward. "You are my assistant today and I'm compensating you well for it. You will be my coffee table." He waved at the space in front of him again. "Here."

There were pivotal moments in my life, moments where I found myself at diverging paths having to make a decision. Did I really want this to be one of my last memories of work? Did I want to let this man use me in such a demeaning way? How much was my pride worth?

The carpet I glared at didn't provide any answers.

I took a deep breath.

This moment wouldn't define me. I could walk out now or later, but later meant a fat paycheck. The coffee would probably fall off my back anyway.

He'd probably make me clean it.

I pushed the shoe-cleaning supplies to the side and crawled over, shifting sideways.

"No," he said.

I glanced up and he twisted his two fingers in the air, motioning for me to turn. I either had to face his groin or give him my ass, and the latter was so not happening. I swiveled around, the short carpet digging into the palms of my hands.

"That's a good girl," he purred, looking down at me

on my hands and knees between his legs. "Just like that."

"I'm a woman, not a girl." Despite my strong words, my heart skipped a beat, and I cursed my own reaction to his comment.

Did I...like his praise?

No.

No, absolutely not.

Last time I checked, I didn't have a praise kink. Yet, when he said "good girl," my body shivered with delight.

Please don't.

"I noticed," he commented, and I momentarily forgot what I'd said for him to respond that way. My mind raced through the conversation. Right. I wasn't a girl, and he'd noticed.

I dropped my head so he wouldn't see my anger and focused on controlling my breath and keeping my back flat. The waistline of my dress pants rubbed against the scar on my hip, but I could maintain this position for a bit.

He didn't move to take his phone out or place his cherished coffee on his human table. He sat there, breathing, glaring at me through a fiery gaze.

"I wonder if you'd suck my cock if the price was right?" he asked.

I bolted up so fast I knocked the coffee from his hand. The cup sailed through the room and splattered against the wall. Black liquid dripped down the off-white paint, making trails to the floor. The smell of coffee filled the air, but I kept my eyes on Mr. Dante.

He stood when I did, towering over me. The cut of his designer suit did a great job of hiding his immense size and strength, but this close, I couldn't possibly ignore the difference in our height and size.

"There you are," he growled. "Finally."

"What?"

"I was wondering how long it would take for you to grow a spine and show your true self."

"What are you talking about? Are you out of your mind?"

His grin grew. "Your demon self."

Oh, so he was bonkers. A complete whacko.

Just perfect. Just fucking perfect. My last well-paying posting that was supposed to fund my bucket list ended up being a sick joke for some lunatic.

Story of my life.

I balled my hands into fists and kicked the shoe-cleaning supplies away from me. "You know what? I don't need a paycheck this badly. I quit."

I spun to leave, but I didn't get very far. I didn't even see him move. One moment, the double doors to freedom were in my sight, and the next, Mr. Dante had me pinned up against the wall beside the splattered remains of his coffee.

He pressed my arms above my head and leaned in close as if to kiss me. Anticipation zinged through my body.

What the fuck?

This is not how I should react to this situation. Some guy had pinned me to a wall, and I reacted with lust instead of rage? I cursed, hating my traitorous body once again.

Not as much as I hated him, though.

"I'm not a demon, you weirdo," I drove my knee up to his groin.

He jerked back and blocked it easily by shifting to the side.

I stomped on his foot.

Nothing.

I kicked his knee and tried to jerk my hands down.

His grip tightened, keeping my wrists exactly where they were, and grinned. "That's right. Let your demon out to play."

He moved my arms so he could hold both wrists in one giant hand and used his other to tug my shirt from my pants.

"Don't touch me, asshole." My mind ran through all the possible maneuvers to get out of his hold, but something in his darkening gaze told me to hold off.

"I'm already touching you." He pressed into my wrists more. "And I'm not enjoying it."

He yanked down on the waistband of my pants, not enough to take them off, just enough to expose the pale skin over my hip bone and the scar from an unfortunate campfire incident.

"This is workplace harassment," I said.

"Go ahead and sue me. You have the mark."

"I have a scar," I clarified. "So what?"

"Look at it."

I twisted to the side and glanced down. Normally a blob with a few lines streaking out, my scar had grown, morphing into an image of a burning flame. "What the hell?"

"Now look at mine." His expression held no lust, only anger danced in his gaze like flames as he ripped his shirt open to expose the scar I'd glimpsed earlier.

Only it wasn't a scar. He had a brand that matched mine.

"The symbol of the damned," he said, loosening his painful grip on my wrists. "The demon brand. All demons carry the mark. Even half breeds like you."

A hysterical laugh bubbled up my throat. This guy was a nut job.

"And let me guess, you're *one hundred percent* demon?" Now that I believed. The rest of this was complete nonsense. "Are all demons such dicks, or just you?"

"Your human half has dulled your senses and watered down your power. I had to push you to see the truth. I will make no apologies for it."

That made no sense. He wasn't even expecting me today. "Is Becca a demon, too, then?"

He surged forward, snaking his hand around my neck so he gripped me by the base of my head. His skin seared mine on contact. "No. She's your friend. I wanted more information on you before we met. But, luckily, I got you instead. And now that you know the truth, you will do as I say."

His words traveled over me, seductive and alluring. I wanted him to keep speaking, to have his deep voice rumble along my skin like phantom fingers.

But the other part of me needed him to get off me and let me go.

I kneed him in the balls.

He didn't have time to block the shot this time. He groaned and bent forward, and in that moment, my training kicked in and I ducked under his arms to break free from his control. I wouldn't stand there and let him manhandle me anymore. I heard what he had to say, and it was absolute garbage.

"Fuck you. I'm done being your servant," I said. "I don't care if we have matching scars. You can go to Hell."

"Interesting choice of words," he muttered under his strained breath, still bent over and leaning against the wall.

He didn't move to chase me, so I slipped out of the office and made a hasty retreat.

A loud roar ripped through the building, shaking the elevator as it carried me to my freedom along with the remaining wad of cash in my pocket. Wow. I'd had a lot of weird jobs in the past, but this one took the cake.

CHAPTER FIVE

I nsane. This entire situation was nothing but pure insanity, and who landed smack dab in the middle of all the craziness? Yup. *Me.*

Like my life wasn't bad enough.

And, normally, I wasn't the type of person to stay down, let alone allow myself to get kicked, but dealing with Mr. Dante threw me off my usual game. I'd let him pin me to a wall, play with my clothes, and spout gibberish instead of kicking his ass. Something about him not only got under my skin but chiseled away my confidence.

And how did I deal with him? By leaving. No asskicking like he deserved.

I kept a hand pressed to the scar on my hip as I hurried home. Hearing the echo of that roar in my ears, I'd hoped he wouldn't come after me. There was only so much I could do against a psychopath like that.

Weird job—no. This went *beyond* weird, and, honestly, the money wasn't worth it no matter what kind of bills knocked at my door.

What kind of crazy man hired a person just to tell them they're a demon? He'd insisted on it, and he hadn't had that kind of zealot glow in his eyes, either. He'd looked perfectly normal.

Yeah, Mr. Dante could definitely go to Hell, but I refused to join him there no matter what kind of lofty claims he threw at me. I'd find another way to get the money I needed without having to degrade myself for someone with more than a few screws loose.

The bills could wait.

I was dying, after all. Maybe I deserved a little break from the constant stress of having to pay to live. I'd take the afternoon, curl up in bed with Chupey and my favorite television shows, and see what I had left in the fridge. Binging on snacks sounded pretty damn good right now.

I made it home in record time and spent precious minutes with my back pressed to the front door trying to drag air into my lungs. Fighting to get my heartrate back to normal. My skin crawled at the memory of the first half of my day.

Closing my eyes, I shook my head, muttering out loud to myself, "I'm not a demon. I'm not a demon. I. Am. Not. A. Demon!"

The scar seemed to throb in silent protest to those words.

Okay. So, maybe I did know something supernatural existed out there. What else would explain my hindsight and above average strength? The idea of a magical world wasn't completely lost on me. But what kinds of creatures were out there? If what Mr. Dante had said was true–if that was his actual name–how did I fit in?

Was there a chance Mr. Dante spoke the truth?

Mom always warned me there were things in the world I might not understand, things most people thought only existed in storybooks. There were creatures lurking in the darkness ready to snap me up and devour me.

Most kids would probably be scared of the boogeyman stories and have trouble sleeping at night.

Mom put me in martial arts to learn how to fight them.

She made sure I could defend myself if those creatures ever came into the light, even though I never saw them. That was probably why I never felt comfortable in a regular, "real person" job. I'd been raised to fight monsters.

It took me way too long to realize that Mom meant my father when she had talked about the supernatural. She didn't just want me to be prepared. She wanted me prepared to fight *him*. The realization hit home around the same time I started to realize that I had special abilities.

Special abilities I definitely didn't use on Mr.

Dante today, no matter how badly he'd deserved a big juicy ass kicking.

I fumbled with my bag, reaching into its depths to try and snag my cell. I needed backup. I needed to tell someone about this.

Becca was unquestionably human and oblivious to magic and even what I could do. I never wanted to bring her into this craziness, but my need to not be alone right now was outweighing my sensibility.

The familiar *click, click, click* of Chupey's nails along the floor greeted me, and I glanced up to see my pooch, his tail wagging in response.

"I know, I'm home earlier than expected. Mom's just having a little freak out, boy," I managed to get out. My smile strained, and I kept digging for my phone.

Please tell me I didn't leave it at that office.

"Give me one second to talk to Becca and then we'll go for a walk. Would you like that?"

Numb fingers finally brushed along the surface of the phone, and I dragged it out before pressing the screen to dial the familiar number.

Yup, I deserved a little meltdown moment. And who better to witness and help me with it than the only friend I had in this world?

Becca answered on the third ring.

"Well?" She sounded excited. "How did it go today? Are you on your lunch break or something? Tell me everything."

I drew in a long, harsh breath. "It...didn't go so well."

"Uh oh." She went quiet.

Yeah, *uh oh* sounded about right.

"What did you do?"

My brows knitted together. "Why do you automatically assume it's me? I'm not the problem this time."

"Because normally you're the one who gets in trouble," Becca retorted smartly.

I gritted my teeth against a swell of anger as I remembered the way Dante had spoken to me. How he'd treated me.

And the way he'd used me for a fucking coffee table.

There were two categories at play in my life: things I'd do for money, and things that were *too* degrading. He'd crossed the line. And I'd let him. I'd stayed there on my hands and knees.

Shame burned inside me.

"Sloane? What happened?" Becca asked.

Did I tell Becca everything? I might as well.

"The man is insane. Utterly and totally insane. I'm not kidding you."

I was still leaning against the door, and I slowly sunk down to the ground. My butt hit the welcome mat and I rested my head on the door. My heartbeat raced in my ears faster than an engine turning over. *Thump, thump, thump.* Any faster and it wouldn't be my mystery illness that killed me. It would be a heart attack.

"You're going to have to elaborate. And try to slow down because you're starting to freak me out."

She didn't sound like it. If anything, she sounded like she was blowing sunshine up my ass and not really worried.

"*You're* freaked out? Girl. Let me tell you this shit."

I went through the entirety of my morning. From start to finish, and everything in between. Right up to the point where he'd touched my scar and made his claims. I made sure to omit the supernatural side of things, namely the morphing, matching scar thing. That was the type of thing you told someone in person. Or took to your grave.

Much to my surprise, Becca began to laugh. "Okay, now I know you're making things up. I'm sure your sexy, hella rich boss did not make you crouch between his legs and shine his shoes."

Although Chupey was the only one around to see my horrified expression, I made it anyway, watching as his head tilted to the side the longer he looked at me. "I'm not making anything up. The dude is seriously deranged. It's good that you didn't take that job because who knows what kind of fucked up crazy shit he might have tried with you. At least I can handle him."

Except I hadn't handled him, had I? Nope, I'd

gotten down on the ground on my hands and knees and became a human end table.

"Honey, I know you've got a lot going on right now," Becca said slowly.

"Yes, that is accurate." I agreed with her.

"It's bound to be wearing on you. I'm surprised you're able to focus on work in the first place. Why don't I come over tonight? I'll bring some stuff and make dinner for us. It might be nice to just have some time alone, the two of us. Without an audience to witness if you need to have a breakdown. Hmm?"

My stomach rumbled in response to the dinner offer, and I shifted my hand to the growling beast below my ribs. I blew out a breath. "Sure. That sounds great. You can also tell me about this mystery guy you're dating."

Becca giggled. "I have *a lot* to tell you. I'll be over at like six. Hold on until then, will you? I'm guessing you're not going back to the job."

I groaned. "You've got that right."

"Okay, well, don't get in any more trouble and I'll see you tonight. Hang in there," she said, disconnecting the call, leaving me with my own thoughts.

Not the most ideal situation.

I set the phone aside and drew my knees up to my chest, staring through them to where Chupey sat. His head still cocked to the side as he watched me.

"I'm freaking out for a good reason," I told him.

"Right? I think it's perfectly rational to not want to work for a guy like that."

I expected a bark for an answer. Maybe a doggy groan or a huff.

I did *not* expect him to open his mouth and tell me in a way too fucking human voice, "Of course not."

My pulsing heart lurched right into my throat along with a killing dose of adrenaline. Screeching, I backed up like the door would suddenly absorb me before scrambling to my feet.

"What the hell?" I screamed.

"Now, don't freak out."

Don't freak out?

Don't freak out?

"I'm definitely freaking out."

My dog sounded way too calm for this situation. Or maybe my disease had gone to my brain and this whole thing was just one last ditch effort cast by my dying neurons.

It was entirely possible.

"Calm down," he said.

"I can't calm down," I snapped. My lungs seized and at once I went lightheaded, black dots dancing in front of my eyes. Was it hot in here? It felt hot in here.

"What am I even doing? Having a conversation with a dog? Like it's a normal, totally not insane thing."

At least my hindsight wasn't tingling. That was a good sign, right?

"It's possible, Sloane. I'm sorry." His lips pulled

back in a fangy smile. "I'm your demonic familiar. Your father sent me ten years ago to watch over you."

This was the end.

I'm dying right now. At this very moment. It was the only explanation.

"Nope. No way."

Sweat clung to my brow as my temper rose. Why was I so damn hot? Like I'd suddenly been dipped in hot oil and fried like a goddamn donut. I tugged at my shirt, desperate for relief, and ended up popping the buttons open at the top instead. It didn't do much to relieve the prickling heat clinging to me except ruin the only dress shirt I owned.

Forcing my body into action, I reached back to the door, grasping for the knob. Although, there was no way I'd be able to outrun the dog if I decided to make a break for freedom. His long, lanky limbs would help him catch up to me in no time, and then he'd use those fangs to take me down.

"I don't even know my father," I said. None of this made sense.

"*Sloane.*"

Why did I get the sense that Chupey was really disappointed in me because of my reaction? I only spoke the truth. My father had exited my life before I made any core memories of him.

"I've always watched over you. From the start," he insisted. "This is not as weird as it seems. Okay?"

"Nope. Sorry. Totally weird." I shook my head. A

thought slammed into my brain, and, through the fear and confusion, anger boiled to the surface. "You let me pick up your shit!"

He did huff then, a very dog-like sound, and rose to slink toward me with his nails clicking. *I should really trim them*, I thought as I stared at him, then nearly burst out laughing.

From the top puff of hair to his whip-like tail, this dog was far from what I'd expect from a demon familiar. Then again, what did I know?

"Your mom kept running, but your father always knew where you were," Chupey said softly. "He's always watched out for you, and when he couldn't, he sent me."

His tongue lolled out from the side of his mouth, and I reached out to give him a pat on pure instinct.

Ooh, I probably shouldn't touch the creature. Should I? Did one pet a demon familiar? Did it matter?

I drew back.

If I really was dying, I might as well lean into something familiar, like petting the dog I found eating garbage from the dumpster behind my apartment building ten years ago. Chupey waited patiently.

I reached out again and scratched behind his ears. When he leaned into the contact and closed his eyes, a sense of calm washed over me.

Maybe this whole talking demon familiar thing wouldn't really change anything. Chupey was still my Chupey.

"It's about time you knew," he finally said with a groan.

I shifted my scratching from one ear to the other. "About how you've been spying on me?"

Everything went from halfway normal—outside of me knowing I was about to die—to topsy turvy in the span of a few minutes. How was that possible?

My biological father apparently cared about my continued existence.

Demonic dog familiars existed.

That meant demons existed.

Another thought twisted my gut. That meant Mr. Dante's claims weren't batshit crazy, like I had originally thought, and I very well could be part demon as he claimed.

Motherfucker.

What else was possible?

A headache bloomed behind my eyes as my mind continued to spiral. Pain squeezed my chest. Either my mystery disease created some serious hallucinations, or this was all real.

"It's about time you know the real reason I'm here with you," he replied. "Not that I haven't loved those homemade peanut butter treats you make. But your dad wanted you to be cared for."

The pain in my chest increased, squeezing the air from my lungs. I'd wanted my father to care for years.

My mother had been tough as nails, but the absence of a second parent had left a hole, an unfulfilled role in my life. Every parent-teacher conference, every family day where classmates proudly held the hands of both parents, every holiday movie, I keenly felt how I was different, how I lacked something in my life that other people had.

This didn't take anything away from Mom. It made me love her more. But her strength couldn't fill that sense of loss whenever my mind dwelled on my absent father. I coped by making him out to be an asshole, the villain. Mom was so scared of him that it wasn't a stretch. It had to be true.

And now to hear he cared? That he'd taken measures to protect me?

It was too much.

"If this is all true, if my father wanted me safe, where is he now?" I asked. "I buried my mother a year ago. Why hasn't he shown up? Where is he?"

Chupey went quiet, and my stomach sank.

Uh oh. Not good at all.

"I don't know," Chupey admitted, his eyes sad and his tail tucked between his legs. "I don't know where he is."

CHAPTER SIX

The roar of a motorcycle ripped down the quiet street outside my apartment building while the moon shone down through my open window. The sweltering heat from the day still lingered in the air and no amount of breeze would relieve me from feeling like a roast left in the oven for three hours too long.

The building manager kept insisting that the air conditioner would be fixed any day now, but at this point, I'd likely keel over before I'd feel the cold bite of artificial air on my skin in my own home.

I sighed and pushed away from the open window. Staring at the stars in the sky would only distract me so long from my very real issues at hand, my most pressing being my need for money. The second was dealing with an overload of information and the feelings that came with them.

After Chupey's big reveal, we'd sat and cuddled on the couch while I read a book and tried to distract my spiraling mind. At some point, I'd ask more questions, but I wasn't ready yet.

Becca had called to delay our dinner date. Her new lover had surprised her with reservations, but she still planned to come over afterward.

I'd believe it when I saw it, but I had to decide how much I wanted to tell Becca. Given more time to calm down and reflect, I no longer thought Mr. Dante was delusional. If demon familiars existed, that meant half-demons—like the guy accused me of being—had to exist, too.

Someone knocked on the door.

I whipped around and studied the solid slab of wood. It didn't give me any answers, but if my door started speaking, I wouldn't be that surprised. Not now.

Unannounced guests rarely showed up at my place. Becca wouldn't be over for another few hours, and the other tenants in the building usually left me alone unless they got drunk or lost their keys and needed me to call the building manager.

It was probably Alice.

I winced. My neighbor across the hall would randomly knock on my door, try to peer over my shoulder and push for an invitation inside. She never got the hint that I liked my privacy. I *liked* being alone.

Having one friend was already pushing my social limits as it was.

In three steps, I made it to the door and looked through the peephole. Ice flowed through my veins and left me shaky.

That wasn't Alice.

Mr. Fucking Dante stood on the other side, looking no less magnificent or arrogant than when I'd met him.

What the hell was he doing here?

Did someone contact him to tell him I needed more misery in my life?

Ugh.

Leaving the safety chain in place, I flipped the deadbolt and opened the door a crack. Now able to see all of him, I wished I'd kept it closed.

He wore black leather boots with silver buckles that matched the chain attached to his straight-cut black jeans and presumably a wallet in his back pocket. Faded along the thighs, the jeans looked well-worn and comfortable, and matched the black shirt with an 80s rock band logo and black leather jacket. He looked like every woman's biker fantasy.

The way he was dressed was the exact opposite of the clean and polished version I'd seen in the office building. But his piercing emerald gaze was the same, and it still threatened to cut me with its intensity.

"What do you want?" I asked.

Mr. Dante smirked and leaned in. "Hell of a way to greet your guest."

"I didn't invite you, so you're not a guest. How did you get my address?" I asked.

Mr. Dante studied the hallway, no doubt taking in the peeling wallpaper and worn carpet. "May I come in?"

"No."

"Would you prefer to discuss things in the hallway for your nosy neighbors to overhear?" He glanced over his shoulder.

On cue, footsteps shuffled behind the door across the hallway. I narrowed my eyes at the other apartment. Alice needed to learn how to mind her own business.

"I don't know you," I told Mr. Dante. "You need to leave."

A smirk tugged at his full lips, and he leaned even closer. The subtle scent of his expensive cologne, along with the smell of leather and gasoline, wafted into my apartment and curled around me seductively. This man had no business looking and smelling as good as he did.

"I don't need your permission to come in. I'm a demon, Sloane. Not a vampire."

"More like pain in my ass."

"Look, I'm trying to be polite and try things the human way here. I know it's what you're used to. Since you've been playing mortal your whole life."

I snorted. Why did that sound like some backhanded comment?

I wasn't fooled.

He talked about mortals as if they were beneath him—beneath us—but how could I not feel mortal, demon or not, when I've been handed a death sentence?

Whatever. I didn't need to listen to this. "You can fuck right off, Dante. Or whatever your actual name is. I'm not letting you in."

I pushed the door, but he reached out lightning-quick and gripped my arm through the small space. With his skin warm on mine, he shouldered his way closer, the chain on the verge of snapping and his face pressed against the door jam.

"Let me in, Sloane." His words flowed over me like smooth butter. Enticing and seductive, his command curled around me. Coaxing me to do just as he demanded. And suddenly, against my own common sense, the urge to step back and open the door seized me. My fingers twitched as the command washed over my skin, taking control of my muscles. I wanted to let him in.

Worse yet, I wanted to take him into my bedroom and let him do all sorts of naughty things to me. I'd do anything to keep him speaking and have that deep rumbling voice caress my skin like a lover's touch.

Horrified, I jerked back and gripped the door tighter, ready to slam it in this asshole's face.

I'd never wanted to punch and kiss someone at the

same time in all my life. Fuck him for making me feel that way. The bastard.

"Let him in, Sloane," Chupey said with a huff from somewhere behind me. It was enough to make me pause. "He's a guardian."

"Am I supposed to know what that means?"

Mr. Dante craned his neck for a better view around me. When he spotted my dog, he smiled. "Chupe, old buddy. Great to see you."

Wait, they knew each other? This was getting weirder by the second.

Chupey hacked as if a hairball had caught in his throat even though he was hairless. "I wish I could say the same, Ryker."

Ryker? The guy's name was Ryker?

As I glanced over my shoulder, he seized the chance and shoved the door open, snapping the chain and throwing me back at the same time.

"Hey!"

Ignoring me, he shouldered his way inside my apartment and kicked the door closed behind him. He crossed the threshold in two long steps and made his way to Chupey who was lounging on the back of the oversized armchair.

Anger spiking, I clenched my fists. What was stopping me from knocking this guy's lights out right now? Then I'd toss his unconscious ass out for Alice to deal with. Or tomorrow's trash collectors.

Glancing at me and then my balled hands at my

side, Ryker said, "What? Do you want to hit me, Sloane?"

"I'd say it's long overdue."

Chupey sighed and shook his head. "Let's not make this any more messy than it already is." He peeked at me, tongue lolling out of the side of his mouth. "Ryker being here can only mean one thing."

"And what's that?" I asked.

Opening his arms wide, Ryker grinned. "Your father is dead."

CHAPTER SEVEN

My apartment was the perfect size for me and Chupey. I knew it was small, but it never felt smaller than it did with Ryker standing in the middle of my living room with his arms stretched out wide, grinning like an idiot. I'd had men over before, but somehow, Ryker had a way of taking up space and stole all the air in the room with his sheer presence.

"My father is dead?" I whispered, not understanding the swirl of thoughts bubbling up from the news. I'd just discovered my father cared enough to protect me, only to find out moments later, he'd died. I turned to Chupey. "Did you know?"

"No." Chupey lowered his head. "I didn't know. Not until now."

I should've been upset, right? Angry, maybe? Hurt?

But all I felt was this heavy emptiness, a void where all my feelings should be. "How? When?"

Ryker dropped his arms and flopped down on the armchair. The cushion moved and Chupey growled before hopping off the back of the chair.

"About a month ago, and I'll spare you the grisly details since we don't know who was responsible. You should've felt the effects of his death," he said and spread his legs out.

I frowned as I tried to think back to a month ago and any strangeness I could remember feeling then. Besides some food poisoning after Chinese food one night, nothing else sprang up from my memory. But I didn't plan to tell Ryker that. "So?"

"So?" Ryker frowned and glanced over at Chupey.

"She doesn't know."

Darkness shadowed Ryker's expression. A mask slid over what had been clear arrogance, leaving something cold and emotionless. "I see."

Chupey turned to me. He plunked his butt down on the rug and lifted his muzzle, so I got a great view of his sharp canines. "Your father was the King of the Underworld."

"Hades?" That...that was kind of badass.

Chupey shook his head. "No, that was your great-grandfather's name. The Immortal Throne has been passed down each generation, but it's not like we announce that shit to mortals, and your father wanted you to have a normal life. He wanted to keep you out of the Underworld."

"Why?"

"Because he loved your mother, and she couldn't survive in his world."

"But why not tell me? Why not know me?" Oh, wow. All the daddy issues were spiraling up for Show-and-Tell.

"He tried. He was in your life when you were little, you just don't remember. One night, when they were both drunk, he showed your mom his powers. She thought he was joking at first, but when you started showing signs of magic and developed the demon mark, she knew he wasn't. When she confronted him, he admitted the truth of who he was."

"As expected, she freaked out and ran," I finished for him. I'd run too if my boyfriend claimed to be the King of the Underworld. "And then he sent you?"

Chupey bobbed his head up and down.

"While this is all very touching," Ryker interrupted with a hard roll of his eyes. "I'm here to deliver this." He reached inside his leather jacket and pulled out a sealed envelope.

I snatched the stiff black envelope from his hand. It was smooth to the touch, and a glob of red wax with a crest sealed the back.

A crest that looked uncomfortably similar to the scar near my hip bone...

I looked up to find Ryker and Chupey watching me intently.

"What's in the envelope?" I asked. And why did the thing feel like it was buzzing in my hands? Vibrating?

"A letter from your father to be delivered upon his death."

"Did you read it?"

Ryker's face twisted as if he'd smelled something foul. "Of course not."

"It's been sealed with dark magic, Sloane," Chupey added, probably trying to be helpful. "No one can open it but you."

Feeling nauseous, I stared at the envelope.

Part of me wanted to tear it open and see what my father—the ruler of Hell—had to say to me after all these years of not knowing him. But the other part... The other part was terrified of the answers I might find.

For years, the only thing I ever knew about my father was that he hadn't been in my life, and he scared Mom.

I tapped the envelope against my palm while my mind spiraled. Chupey and Ryker's prying stares weren't helping.

With a shake of my head, I slipped the envelope onto the kitchen counter. Now wasn't the time. I'd read it later, in private.

Turning back to the living room, I found Ryker and Chupey still studying me with that unnerving stillness.

"Thanks for delivering the letter." I waved at the door to give Ryker a not-so-subtle hint. It was time for him to pack it up and get the hell out of my home. "Let me show you out."

He grunted and leaned back on the couch. He man-spread as if he owned the space around him and gripped the chain on his jeans with one hand to play with the links. "I'm also here to formally invite you to take your place as Lucifer on the Immortal Throne."

My mind went completely blank. As if someone wiped the hard drive of my brain, all the thoughts whirling around in my head fled at Ryker's words.

He didn't look happy about giving the invitation, either. His posture might've been relaxed, but he bit the words out and his gaze had that hard glare I now expected every time he looked at me.

"Take my place?" I whispered. Surely, I heard him wrong. "Wait, Lucifer?"

"You are to cross the Styx and present yourself to the Council of Six in two weeks. I highly suggest you embrace your demonic nature and gain mastery over your unique powers by then." He didn't look at me while he spoke. Instead, he continued to play with the silver chain, the artificial apartment lights glinting off the shiny surfaces.

"My unique powers?" My thoughts immediately

went to my hindsight. Had that been the demon part of me all along? Guessed so.

He nodded, still not looking up. "Every demon has a special talent. You've repressed your demon side for twenty-five years, so if it's not evident by now, there may be a problem."

Crossing my arms across my chest, I scoffed. "Oh, there's no problem."

"If I had to guess? Your power is annoying people."

This guy had some balls on him. Seriously.

"And if I had to guess, your special talent is being an asshole." I snapped back. Apparently, I wasn't above playing his childish games.

That's right, hit me below the belt and I'll drop down to your level.

"He controls by touch," Chupey answered despite Ryker and my bickering. "Bend the wills of others to do whatever he wants."

"Wait...like mind control?"

Ryker shrugged as if it was no big deal. Meanwhile, I felt like all the oxygen had been sucked out of my lungs.

I madly shuffled through my memories of every second we'd been together. Like in his office and before by the door. When he had touched me... When he had forced me to scrub his fucking shoes...

When he was pretending to be my boss, he'd held me to the wall and, instead of fighting, I'd let him pin me there and got mildly turned on.

I winced. Maybe a little more than mildly turned on.

Had that all been because I was under his influence? His *power*?

"You *sonofabitch!*" Fury lashing through me, I leapt across the room and let the punch I'd been holding since I met him fly. Somehow, he turned at the last minute. I clipped his jaw hard enough to snap his head to the side.

He sprung to his feet, towering over me. My hindsight wailed while anger blazed in his gaze. "You punched me?"

Well, I tried to punch him, and now he tried to make me cower beneath him. I'd gone toe-to-toe with guys three times his size in the ring, so he was going to have to do more than that to intimidate me. "Yeah, and I'm about to do it again if you don't back off."

He didn't move. Instead, he seethed and glared at me with narrowed eyes. Challenging me. I met it head-on, refusing to break the eye contact. I didn't even blink.

"Okay, now," Chupey said after a long moment. "Enough of this. There's still a lot that we need to get through. We've only scratched the surface here for Sloane."

Still, Ryker didn't budge. Only his lip curled up over clenched teeth and a growl rumbled in his throat. An actual *growl*.

"Ryker—" Chupey chastised. "Stand down."

His hardened gaze danced over my face, debating.

Chupey barked. "Ryker!"

"Fine!" He ripped himself away and crossed the room to the opposite side, where he spun on his heel, his shoulders tense. "But if she hits me again, I swear—"

"If I hit you again, I'll make sure you won't get up," I said, anger still fueling me. "Especially after you used your power on me."

"You're overexaggerating. It didn't even work."

I paused as my temper deflated all around me. "It... didn't?"

Chupey's little head swiveled my way and the little bastard winked.

Drawing in a deep breath, I tried to settle my frantic heartbeat. This was beginning to be too much. Demons, Hell, my father, a throne, powers...? This was like some fever dream I desperately wanted to wake up from. Now.

I glanced between the two of them, my neurons firing rapidly but somehow unable to string together the right words to make a coherent sentence. "Uh, what? Wait, how—I...?"

"Oh shit, I think we broke her." Ryker laughed, and it only made me want to punch him again, this time in that stupid gorgeous, sculpted chest.

Clearing my throat, I tried again, making sure to direct the question to Chupey. "*How* is that possible?"

"Because I went easy on you," Ryker interrupted with an annoyed huff.

"Explain."

"I didn't really try to control you. Not really," he said. "You're a demon with natural defenses, so it would require more effort on my part to control you with my power. What the fuck does it matter anyway? You need to focus on the challenges for the throne."

"Challenges?" I asked.

"Are you fucking deaf? Yes, challenges."

Now he was speaking my language. If this was a physical fight kind of thing, I had this in the bag. Although... supernatural demonic powers might make things a little more difficult. More *interesting*. But a little competition never scared me. "And what happens then?"

"You will have to pass a set of trials, collectively referred to as the Inferno," he replied, adjusting his leather jacket with a quick shrug of his shoulders.

"Trials? Plural?" Okay, so not a fight. "As in tests?"

"You could say that."

I glanced at Chupey again for some kind of confirmation, and the dog dipped his head in a nod.

My pulse instantly picked up. One thing I had never been good at in school was taking tests. Projects, sure. Speeches, that was pie. But tests? Nope.

The more I thought about it, the more my stomach soured. "Yeah, no thanks. I'm going to have to pass."

Ryker stilled and blinked at me, shock and disbelief all over his expression. "Excuse me?"

"You heard me. I'm not interested in taking a test."

"This isn't the SETs, Sloane," he hissed. "These challenges are designed to prove you are ruthless and brutal enough to rule the pits of Hell."

I snorted a laugh. "First, it's SATs, and second, ruthless and brutal? I'm not either of those things, so I'd fail right there."

"You are in the cage."

My muscles tightened at that. Had he been...*watching* me?

I don't know why, but a delicious tingle shot down my spine at the idea. "And how do you know that?"

He opened his mouth to answer, but Chupey yipped to steal our attention again. "We're getting off-topic again." His head whipped my way. "Sloane, this is bigger than you realize. You need to think about it first, really think about it, before you go making rash decisions like this."

"Why the hell would I want anything to do with a father who wanted nothing to do with me? I don't know anything about the Underworld. I didn't even know demons existed, and now I'm expected to rule them? I want nothing to do with the throne."

A slow smile spread across Ryker's face, one that was calculated and full of secrets. Like him. Before I could realize what was happening, he grabbed my hand for a firm shake. "Can I get that in writing?"

"Don't you dare try to use your special touchy-feely powers on me." Disgusted, I attempted to tug my arm back, but he held on and then lifted my hand to his face. His warm lips pressed against the scarred, rough skin of my knuckles.

"I can't say it's been a pleasure."

Ugh. I snapped my hand back and this time he let go. Wise, since I planned to kick him in the balls if he tried to hold on any longer.

Pulling my shoulders back, I pinned Ryker with my best death glare. "I hope you burn in Hell."

His gaze brightened and for a second it looked as though green flames flickered in his eyes. "Oh, I plan to."

I watched as Ryker Dante walked out, and as soon as the door shut, Chupey rushed across the room and bumped into my legs.

"That was a mistake, Sloane," he growled.

"Geez, Chupey." Rolling my eyes, I grabbed a beer from the fridge and popped off the lid. "Tell me how you really feel." Then I realized just how ridiculous all of this was and took two huge gulps of my drink. I mean, I was arguing with my dog about taking over the Underworld, for fuck's sake.

When my gaze fell on the letter that Ryker had handed me again, I grunted, still not wanting to read the thing yet. If ever.

Not today, Satan.

Literally.

"Sloane, listen to me. You're letting your daddy issues get in the way of your success. Of your life."

I choked on the beer. Instead of spraying the pale ale all over Chupey and my dinette set, I swallowed it down with a whole bunch of air. The bubble traveled down my throat and settled as a painful lump in my stomach.

"Not... fair," I sputtered.

Chupey cocked his head at me, his one ear pointing straight up at the ceiling. "You told me to be honest. I was honest. I don't understand mortals, sometimes."

Mortal. I've never felt more mortal than I did right now. Sure, my biological sperm donor was the King of the Underworld, but all that gave me was a tingling sense of danger and some asshole knocking on my door. Last I checked, I was still dying, and this changed nothing.

"You need to claim the throne," Chupey went on. "It's what your father would want."

"I don't care what he would want. I didn't know him, remember?" I flopped down on the couch, momentarily distracted by the scent of Ryker's cologne that still clung to the worn fabric. I inhaled deeply. That man smelled like sin in all the right ways. "Besides, there's no point."

Chupey jumped up on the cushion beside me and sat. "What do you mean?"

"I'm dying, Chupey," I said. The words almost got

stuck in my throat, but he had the right to know. I couldn't exactly take him to that no-kill shelter anymore. Not with him talking and all...demonic like he was.

When Chupey blinked at me and didn't immediately fill the silence, I kept going. "The doctors don't know what's wrong with me, only that my organs are all failing. They've given me about a month, but there are a lot of unknowns."

He didn't say anything for a while. Instead, he stared at me, wagging his tail like a normal dog would, and in those few moments, I struggled to remember he was so much more than that.

When he finally spoke again in a human voice, that was where the sense of normalcy evaporated.

"Of course, you're dying. You're half demon. Your human half and demonic half are fighting with each other, and this isn't a war where there's a winner. The halves will both fight until you die."

The neurons in my brain misfired. "What?" That was absurd—just as absurd as everything else had been today—but he said it as if it were a fact. A fact that was as clear as fucking day. "No way. Is that possible?"

Chupey whined and ducked his head. "I knew you were sick, but you never told me how sick. I thought maybe it was a cold or something typical for your mortal species. You didn't tell me it had progressed to something life-threatening."

"You're my *dog*. I didn't think I needed to tell you this kind of stuff."

"And not knowing about your father's passing, I thought we had more time," Chupey continued.

"Time for what?" I asked.

"Everything," he replied. "Time to explain everything."

"You had ten years."

He looked away.

My thoughts didn't stop spinning in my head. "Is my condition somehow tied to my father's death?"

"He was protecting you in more ways than one."

"How," I demanded, beer forgotten.

"He sent me, which you already knew, but he also laid a spell to keep your demon nature in stasis. With him gone, though, his magic can no longer protect you." He lifted his paw and set it on my lap. Though he was a demon, he had no qualms about giving me that puppy-dog look—the super sad and pathetic one that used to get him extra treats. "You will perish if you do not take the Immortal Throne and become a full demon."

I set the beer down on the table beside the couch. "And claiming the throne is the only way to do that?"

"Can I be brutally honest?"

"You mean you weren't before?"

"You're dying and you're broke. What more do you have to lose?"

Well, when he put it like that...

CHAPTER EIGHT

Chupey was right.

I really didn't have anything to lose at this point, and the thought of traveling to the Underworld didn't turn my blood to ice. Instead, a sense of wonder gripped me. What would the Underworld look like? Smell like? Would I burst into flame?

No amount of alcohol was going to help me feel calmer or more grounded. I put the beer down and ran through my options. Either I head to the unfamiliar demonic world I didn't know existed until today, or I waste away in the mortal realm and count down the hours until I died. And if I did die, would I end up in Hell anyway? Was this entire thing just unavoidable?

I heaved a sigh and said, "I have more questions."

"Of course, you do," Chupey replied with a short nod. "It's expected after... *everything*."

"If I say no—for real—I'll definitely die?"

"Definitely. Your demon side can't coexist with your mortal one on this plane. It will destroy you."

Well, shit. "And if I do die...won't I just go to Hell anyway? My soul or whatever? Isn't that how it works?"

Chupey's thin lips lift to expose his fangs. "No. The idea of humans dying and going to Heaven or Hell is a religious-based one, but those places, angels and demons, they're just other supernatural creatures, ones that live in different realms."

"So, dying means...I'm just dead?"

"The dead serve to fuel magic. That is all. It doesn't matter what kind of being—mortal, demon, or otherwise. We all become fuel before we're reborn."

In other words, dead still meant dead. Being part demon wasn't going to change that. My only hope was this Immortal Throne and becoming a full demon.

But trials? In Hell?

My mother might've been afraid of my father and what he was, but if she knew I was dying, she'd tell me to fight. Fight like she did and never give up. She fought for her life until the very end.

And that was just what I was going to do too.

Mama didn't raise no bitch.

I slapped my hands down on my thighs, making up my mind. "Okay, I'm in. What do I need to do? How do we do this?"

"I'll help you," Chupey answered. "But you have to be absolutely sure this is what you want."

"Yeah. Sure. I don't want to die, right? And since this is the only way to save me, I'll do it." Not because of my father and any unresolved daddy issues I undoubtedly had, and not because of Ryker. I was doing this for *me*. Me. And that was it. "What do we need to do?"

And would I actually be able to do it? My father had put me in some sort of magical stasis. Had I become magically stunted as well as oblivious? Would things have been different if he'd let me develop naturally, with my demon side out in full view instead of stuffed down somewhere inside of me?

Thinking about the unknowns wouldn't help me right now, but this definitely seemed like the sort of thing to cause an existential crisis later.

"You're going to have to use your blood," Chupey interrupted my thoughts. "You'll draw a sacred symbol and whisper an incantation to open up the portal to Hell and your blood acts as the key to open it. Once we've done that, we'll step through and boom. Done."

Somehow, I just knew things weren't quite that simple.

My stomach swirled at the thought of what I was about to do, but I managed to nod. "Let me grab a knife from the kitchen. I'm guessing it doesn't have to be something fancy?" I asked. "Any sharp object will do as long as I bleed for it?"

He woofed instead of saying anything else.

"Are you sure you're not actually a dog?"

"I'm a Chupacabra." He sounded indignant.

I took my jelly legs and shaky hands into the kitchen and grabbed the sharpest knife from the holder on the countertop. Old, with a rusted handle, the knife could slice a fingertip with enough pressure.

Standing between Chupey and the couch, I thrust out a hand with the knife poised above my skin. "Well?"

"Draw the blade over your palm. You need at least ten drops or so." Chupey bent to scratch at a spot near the scruff of his neck.

"Just, like, right here?"

Chupey paused his scratching. "Like, totally."

I pushed aside my irritation. This was it. No going back. I might not believe entirely about this whole demon stuff, but I had to take the next step forward.

I fully planned to go to Hell one way or another.

Holding an overheated breath in my lungs for five seconds, ten, I ran the tip of the knife through my skin until it bit deep.

"What's the sigil?"

"Same as the symbol and seal of the damned," he said.

"Like my scar?"

"Exactly."

Chupey then told me the words to repeat for the incantation and my lips parted but nothing came out of my mouth.

Licking my lips, I tried again, repeating the words

and drawing the symbol on the floor while my demon dog licked his balls beside me.

Chupey stopped mid-lick and settled his black gaze on me. "You need to pour your magic into it."

"How?"

He cocked his head. "I don't know. It's something that comes naturally to demons. Try pulling some feelings out." He went back to cleaning himself.

"I should've had you fixed," I muttered. Irritation flashed through me, remembering everything I'd been through today. Chupey was such a shit.

The sigil might not be the prettiest but at least it looked decent. I'd bled for it. I kept repeating the words, closing my eyes and trying to reach deep inside myself for the demon magic supposedly inside me.

If Chupey thought I could do this, then I had no choice but to actually do it.

I closed my bleeding hand into a fist against the sharp sting of pain from my cut. "Why isn't it working?" I said through gritted teeth.

Magic began to spark and fizzle from the sigil I'd drawn on the floor. Huh. Anger? Was anger the right fuel? Well then, no problem, because I had plenty to be pissed about.

I turned up the heat on my glare a notch as I stared down at the floor imagining Ryker's face and channeling every shitty thing that had happened to me. Lack of a father figure, Mom dying, my own diagnosis, my poverty. The angrier I felt, the larger the halo of magic grew until it was large enough for a man—or in this case, a badass bitch—to step through.

The edges of the portal glowed in shades of blue and gold with the center shimmering and solid.

Chupey trotted over to my side on those long legs. "Let's do this."

It wasn't until we stepped through the portal that I remembered Becca coming over later with food, a shoulder to cry on, and gossip about her new lover.

Oops.

If she actually showed, she was going to be pissed to find my place empty.

The magic swept over my shoulders like a warm blanket. Growing warmer by the second, I thought, the magic spitting us out into a room made of black stone.

Chupey panted. When he looked up at me, he froze. "Huh, red."

"What are you talking about?"

"Your hair."

I grabbed a chunk of hair and held it in front of my face. Even in the dark room, with only the nearby torches providing a soft glow of light, there was no mistaking the vibrant red of my hair. Far brighter and far redder than the mousy brown it had been moments ago. "What the fuck, Chupey?"

"Welcome to the Underworld," he said.

I blinked and an awkward laugh bubbled out of my mouth. A change in hair color was the least of my concerns right now. I had to let it go for now and freak out about it later.

"I wouldn't have made it without my faithful canine companion," I said.

Chupey wagged his tail.

Were all Chupacabras like this or had he pretended to be my dog for too long that these things were becoming second nature for him?

Never mind. Like my hair, it was something that could wait. I had more important things to worry about now. Like figuring out where I was.

I turned and scanned my new surroundings, and well...*damn*.

The entire grand room was made out of black stone with a river of molten magma coursing through its center and nearly cutting the space in half. Walls made of shining black obsidian rose up so high, the ceiling remained hidden in the shadows above. Torchlight illuminated the carvings on the walls, the flickering fire making the images come to life and appear as though they moved. At the far side of the large room, a huge vacant throne waited.

My father's throne.

This place stole my breath and my voice away.

"Come on." Chupey whined to get my attention before taking a few steps forward. "It's time to show you your new digs."

New digs, sure.

I stifled my smile at the thought and followed Chupey.

"I thought Ryker said we'd have to pass over the Styx to get to the Underworld," I said.

He shot me a doggy version of a shrug. "Maybe for amateurs. Not for you. We've traveled directly into the throne room."

For a dog, or demon familiar, he seemed pretty pleased with this. Maybe I'd accomplished something big, but I barely managed to smile back at him, the effects of adrenaline already beginning to fade, threatening to leave me exhausted. "So, if my father was Lucifer, what will I be called when I take the throne?"

"Lucifer is just a title," Chupey told me when we stepped farther into the cavernous space and toward the throne carved from black rock. Sheer spikes rose from the back with curved armrests. The entire piece was made up of one seamless stone with a wall of skulls rising up behind it in a macabre backdrop.

"It's not a person, nor is the title gender specific," Chupey continued. "So, you will also be Lucifer."

My stomach twisted at the sight of that throne. The seat of Hell. Technically, it was my royal ass that was supposed to sit on it and here I stood, my jaw gaping open and my eyes wide.

My father had once sat there. He'd sat on this very throne, wheeling and dealing and doing whatever it was that a ruler of literal Hell did. "Shock" put it mildly. None of this felt real. I'd stepped into madness, or a parallel dimension where the impossible became very clearly possible.

"Like a monarch's title," I finally replied, addressing Chupey's one-sided discussion on the title of Lucifer.

He nudged me again and I took one step, then another, toward that throne. My past and my present collided inside of me like a clash of fists.

"Exactly," Chupey agreed. "Your father *was* Lucifer. And his father before him, down the line. So, you have a legitimate claim to be the next Lucifer."

I shivered under the weight of those words. *The next Lucifer.* Was that something I actually wanted or just what was expected of me?

I swallowed the irritation.

It was this or death.

"Your claim is being challenged," Chupey continued. His voice echoed strangely across the throne room, and I wondered if there was no one else around. "The trials start tomorrow."

"Tomorrow?" I froze. "I thought I had two weeks."

"Not anymore."

I blinked at him. "Wait. How did you find any of this out? How do you know where my room is? You've been with me this entire time."

Chupey huffed and looked away.

"Chupey!"

"I can communicate telepathically with other familiars when I'm in the Underworld. I just found out about the trials, okay?" He snorted. "And now my head is full of excited voices, but no one knows anything more, or if they do, they're not the ones talking. All I know is the Inferno starts tomorrow."

Ryker. His pretty face flashed in my mind, and I instantly wanted to smash something. He'd set me up. If I had taken two weeks to get here, I would've missed the Inferno altogether.

I stopped walking and took a deep breath, trying to center myself.

I still wore my white shirt from work today with the missing buttons. Still wore the pressed pants and shoes and part of me felt like I should be giving tours of this place rather than contemplating if I had what it took to rule it.

"Are you okay?" Chupey asked.

"I wasn't aware a throne existed until today. And if my father was..." I couldn't even say the word. "It makes sense the power vacuum created some healthy competition with his absence."

"Healthy or not, there is competition."

"You don't need to tell me twice," I muttered. But how did he know for sure my claim was challenged? He didn't sound like he was guessing. More chatter in his head with the other familiars?

Apparently, Chupey felt he did, in fact, need to tell me twice, because he kept going, explaining things to me as if I was a child.

Maybe to him, I was.

According to Chupey, if I wanted this throne, if I actually wanted my father's title, I had to push myself to the limit and deal with others doing the same.

What kind of creatures would be battling for my father's throne?

The thought stumped me. Well, actually, two specific words did.

My and *father*.

I hadn't had a lot of time to process all the information I'd received tonight, including my father's death and what that meant exactly. Oh, I knew I had to fight for his throne, but the personal implications were harder to wade through. I never knew my father, and now I had to accept I never would.

Chupey stood still, ears pinned back, the hair on the top of his head bristling as the sound of footsteps from behind us.

"Normally we charge for gawking, but I guess in this case we can make an exception," a male voice called out. Followed by a completely out-of-place laugh.

I turned to find a demon standing a few feet away with sharp snow-white colored horns curling above his ears and on top of his head. He wore head-to-toe black leather that clung to sculpted muscles and left his arms bare. He had a dagger strapped to one thigh and held a nasty looking spear in one hand. When his eyes, no more than red slits, settled on me, I took an automatic step in the opposite direction.

A demon.

A real demon stood in front of me.

I guess I still hadn't come to terms with being one myself.

My hindsight tingled, the same ones that kept me winning my fights in the Underground. *Danger, danger!*

No shit.

"Just taking in the sights," I said with forced ease.

Chupey shifted to my side, but he wasn't growling, which spoke in the demon's favor, at least.

"What do you think of the place?" The guy gestured toward the throne, his leather bodysuit creaking from the movement. "I bet it's a lot to take in, right? And all of this is yours!"

"I'm not sure I'd call it mine yet, but I'm definitely —" *Do not tell him that you're overwhelmed,* "adjusting."

There. It felt like a good compromise.

"I'm Zane, one of the demons in your father's old guard. And if you need anything during your stay here, please don't hesitate to call me."

I wanted to jump out of my skin at that. "You knew my father?"

"Sure did. As well as anyone could know Lucifer." Zane gestured toward the raised dais holding the throne. When I didn't move right away, he walked over, rested his spear on the steps and sat down. He patted the dark stone beside him.

I had options.

I could walk or run away. I could remain standing at a safe distance.

But none of these other options would get me answers.

With a deep sigh, I walked over and perched my butt on the edge of the step. Chupey plopped his ass down between us and my hand fell automatically to his hairless back. My fingers ran along something hard and spiky. I gasped and snapped my hand away. Instead of Chupey's normally smooth back, bony spikes protruded from his spine.

Chupey thumped his tail on the steps. "Told you I was a Chupacabra."

I snorted and rubbed circles along his side, avoiding the spines, like I used to. Before all this demon craziness.

No matter what my instincts told me about staying on guard, I wanted to know more about my father and this place. I craved it, the way some people did their morning coffee. This demon had known my father. He knew more than I did about the man who had sired me. More than my mother had ever been willing to divulge outside those unspoken words when she forced me into self-defense classes.

"Your father wasn't an easy man. Of course not, because he reigned over the Underworld. He was brutal and vicious, but not without reason."

I groaned. "Not really helping me feel any better, Zane."

The demon shook his head before saying, "You look like him, you know. You have the same features."

"Funny, I've always been told I look exactly like my mom."

"By those who never knew your father, maybe. But you've got his smile, too. And from the stories that have reached us of your fighting, then you also have his bloodthirsty resolve to win at all costs. It's an admirable trait."

Maybe down here it was. Not so sure it could help me out in the living realm. That kind of stuff was normally frowned upon.

"Wait a minute. Who has been telling stories about me?" I asked. Then, I narrowed my eyes and turned on my dog.

He apparently had a more active social life than I did.

Chupey glanced away.

"Not much has reached us, mind you. Only stories of your victories. How you've demolished your opponents with a single hit," Zane continued.

"Not completely true, but thank you," I said, while Chupey remained suspiciously quiet. When I turned to the demon again, he was smiling wide with pointed teeth and with admiration. My chest warmed. He was proud of me—actually proud of me—and for all those times I fought and won in the Underground.

It was nice to have that kind of recognition. I hated to admit it, but between Mom and Becca's obvious disapproval, I'd been craving it for a long time.

Unexpectedly, Zane jumped to his feet again. "Come on. There's much more to tell and show you before the Inferno begins. It's time you learn about your true home."

I stood too, but on wobblier legs. Even my head was light, but not from a mystery sickness. From...well, from *everything*.

I'd been given so much information, and in an instant, my world had been turned on its head. I'd gone from thinking I was dying to finding out Hell was real, my father was Lucifer, a king, and I had to compete for the throne to save myself, a throne Ryker wanted as well. Then I'd discovered that after all these years of thinking my father didn't give two shits about me, he'd been protecting me, missing me, *loving* me, from afar. Oh, and let's not forget that my garbage eating, butt-scratch loving rescue dog was a fucking Chupacabra and I was a demon.

Okay, half demon. But still.

It was...*a lot*.

I swayed on my feet and instantly felt Chupey's fuzzy head push against my leg, as if he was trying to help me stay upright.

"Careful, there," Zane said, brow crinkling with concern. "Take it easy."

"She's been through a lot," Chupey added. "Maybe

I should just show her to her room and let her rest a bit. We can have a tour another time."

"No!" The word snapped from me. I wanted to see more. I needed to. "This is a part of myself I've waited forever to know about. I'm fine. Just tired."

It was the understatement of the century, and from the looks of disbelief on both their faces, they knew I was full of it too.

As strong as I liked to think I was, the weight of everything was finally catching up to me, and I was beyond overwhelmed. But I was also stubborn as hell. "Zane, tell me more about my father. And this place— it's huge. I want to see it all."

Chupey's disapproving growl rumbled beside me, but I ignored it.

"I'll rest later," I told him.

"A quick tour then, Zane. The main rooms only," the demon dog instructed. "That's it."

Zane nodded and strolled ahead, leading us out of the throne room and into an equally as grand space with a dining table as long as a tennis court with seating for at least fifty guests.

Did they have parties down here? It was hard to imagine a bunch of horned and spikey demon creatures sitting down for tea or having polite conversation.

"You know..." Chupey began as Zane led us into a grand foyer with a peaked ceiling and black crystal chandelier, "Demons are just a different supernatural type really. At least that's how we see it. We don't collect damned souls or feed on the sinful or anything like that."

I jerked my head his way. "Can you read my mind or something?"

He snorted. "No, but I've lived with you long enough to guess what you're thinking."

Uh huh. I'm not sure if I believed that.

"He's right," Zane answered. "We live in this realm because we have to. Our bodies can't stay in the living world too long. But we lead normal lives considering."

"So all the torture and punishments for our living sins were always just stories?" I asked. "What about the fire and brimstone?"

Zane chuckled, his thick shoulders bouncing. "Stories? Those are just a typical Tuesday night!"

Unsure if he was joking or not, I let out a nervous laugh and glanced at Chupey. But his expression wasn't reassuring.

This place was not what I was expecting. At all.

Peering up the beautiful black marble staircase, I asked, "Are we going upstairs next?"

Zane shook his head. "Not yet. There's one more thing I want to show you." He tilted his spear toward a small alcove beside the steps.

"What is it?" But as I strode over, I got my answer. A massive oil painting hung against the wall—at least ten feet tall—of a man wearing polished black armor. For some reason, my next breath froze in my chest. Surprisingly, it wasn't because of the three-eyed skull in his hand or the amount of blood splattered across his medieval inspired outfit.

No, it was because of the way his dark eyes peered down at me. As if he could see me and my very presence would magically fill him with life so he could step right off the canvas. The details were lifelike—disturbingly so—and as I scanned his shoulder-length hair and thin face, I recognized similar features there too. The shape of his nose, high cheekbones, and peaked hairline. The most striking one was in the quirked smile he wore.

Just like Zane had said.

I whirled around on the demon guard. "Wait. Is this—Is this my dad?"

He was grinning again, loving that I had figured it out. "Yes, it is."

Stepping closer to the portrait, my heart beat a little faster. Really, I was staring at a stranger; I'd never met this man in my life, yet he felt familiar, like a part of myself recognized him.

It was unnerving.

"See? You look like him," Zane said. "Do you see it now?"

A little, yeah. But he definitely looked more like a *Lucifer* than I did.

"How...did he die?" I started carefully. It was a question I'd been wondering but was too afraid to ask.

When Zane opened his mouth to reply, Chupey

jumped in between us and yipped. "That's a story for another day."

"What? Why?"

Zane nodded. "Right. Agreed."

"Why can't I know?"

"Later," Chupey barked sharply.

Before I could argue more, the two of them headed for the stairs, cutting my curiosity short.

Why the secrecy around his death? I didn't understand.

Relenting, I followed my two guides upstairs. Guess I'd have to wait for that one.

CHAPTER NINE

Back in my small apartment, I placed my empty mug on the counter and leaned forward to rest my forehead on the cupboard. It felt good to return to a familiar place. The last few hours left me feeling as though someone had pulled out the rug from under my feet and left me to flail in the air.

Wait. When had I returned to my apartment?

Strong hands gripped my waist and slid down my short, silk nightie to rest on my hips.

Nightie?

Silk?

Okay, this had to be a dream. But a nice one for once.

I didn't want to wake up.

The man standing behind me leaned in, his chest pressing into my back, his warmth caressing my skin.

His hot mouth found my neck and he lay lazy kisses along my exposed shoulder.

"Are you sure you want to be my enemy?" Ryker's deep voice vibrated over my body. "We could be so much more as friends."

Instead of spinning around to punch him in the throat, I purred and arched into him, rubbing my ass into his groin, feeling his stiff erection.

This most definitely had to be a dream, but I had no intentions of trying to stop it. I liked this feeling of closeness, or intimacy too much, even if it did star my most hated enemy.

Ryker growled, his fingertips digging into my skin. He spun me around, picked me up and sat me on the counter. His gaze smoldered and he gave me a whole second to appreciate his beauty before he snagged my lips in a kiss that stole my breath away. His hands traveled up my thighs, slipping the silk nightie higher and higher up my legs until it bunched at my waist.

Huh.

I wasn't wearing any panties. Thank God for the magical wonders of dreams.

Ryker abandoned my lips and kissed his way down my throat and chest, pulling down the straps of the nightie along the way. The silky material slipped down to pool at my waist. His hot mouth captured a nipple and I gasped. Threading my hands through his soft hair, I gripped his head and held him in place as he teased me with his tongue.

"Not enough," he growled. "I need more."

He leaned down and scooped me up. I might be fit from all my training and fighting in a cage, but I wasn't little. I wasn't light or someone easily tossed around. This didn't phase Dream Ryker for a second. He hoisted me up and walked out of the kitchen to throw me against the wall. I draped my legs over his shoulders and suddenly his mouth was at my core and he was finding new ways to tease me with his tongue.

Nipping, sucking and licking, he stoked a fiery need burning inside me. Pleasure built, threatening to erupt. He reached over with his free hand to press down–right there, right on the perfect spot–while he plunged his tongue inside me.

My world exploded, pleasure rippled through me while I clutched his hair and my thighs clamped his head to keep him in place.

I lurched awake, pleasure still rippling through me.

Holy shit... That *dream.*

It had been both terrifying and mind-numbingly hot at the same time. Invisible ropes tightened around my lungs and squeezed. The aftershocks of my dream orgasm faded quickly, though, replaced with panic as the events of the last twenty-four hours came crashing back.

What the hell had I gotten myself into?

After the quick tour, Zane had led me to one of the billion bedrooms to sleep in for the night. He had apologized for the plainness of it and assured me the suite

Lucifer stayed in was much nicer, but really, I was flabbergasted by the sheer size and extravagance of it. Damn place was nicer than my apartment with a queen-sized bed, a full bathroom with claw-foot tub and standing shower, and a lush, shag carpet that felt like heaven on my feet. A massive arched window took up most of the far wall, and through the stained-glass pieces, I could just make out the outline of a body of water. Or maybe it was magma. It was hard to tell with so much darkness clinging to the sky.

Did it always look like it was about to thunderstorm here?

The comfort of the bedroom almost made me forget what I was up against here. Win the crown or die. Me, a half human going up against much stronger and scarier demons. The only thing I had going for me was that I was used to taking down bigger opponents than me. I had made a living off it.

I just had to hope it'd pay off here, too.

Meanwhile, my demon dog familiar had left me to *pop* back to the mortal realm and grab some of my stuff. Apparently, Chupacabras could move between the realms with ease in addition to communicating telepathically with other familiars in the Underworld. How Chupey planned to pack my stuff without opposable thumbs confused and intrigued me at the same time.

My door was flung open, and Zane sauntered into the room holding boots in one hand and a bunch of black cloth in the other. He wore skin tight leather pants that hugged his muscular thighs and a matching sleeveless vest that showed off his arms. The demon was jacked.

I sat up and rubbed my eyes. "Um...hello? Have you heard of knocking?"

"You need to get dressed." He tossed the black material onto the bed beside me and kicked the door closed behind him. With a flick of his wrist, he flung the black combat boots in my direction. They tumbled on the ground beside the bed.

"Are you planning to watch?" I narrowed my eyes.

His unsettling red-slit gaze focused on me. "I plan to guard you and, once you're decent, escort you to the throne room."

Well, Chupey hadn't returned yet, so some backup in an unfamiliar place would be welcome, but the idea of needing a guard while I got naked had panic squeezing my lungs again.

I picked up the strap of one of the pieces of clothing and held it up. The thing has more holes in it than my target at the range. "Define decent?"

"Just put it on."

"Fine." I slipped from the bed and held my hand up, rotating my fingers in a circular motion. "But turn around."

"Honey, you're not my type."

"Well, my type is modest."

Zane sighed dramatically, flinging his long hair so it

tangled with his horns, and turned around, the leather pants doing wonders for his ass.

"So why am I not your type?" I asked. "Is it the half-human thing?"

"It's the vagina thing."

I snorted and held the black shirt up to examine it. The ripped clothing wasn't exactly what I had in mind for battling demons over a throne. I chucked it on the bed and sighed. "While I'm shoving my body parts into this contraption, tell me more about the Inferno."

"There's nothing more to tell," he huffed.

"Then go over it again." I pulled off my tank top and flung it on the bed. "Please."

"The Inferno is comprised of six trials, each representing one of the six domains of Hell. Each member of the council is responsible for designing a trial that will test a key attribute of a strong, successful leader. Which trial will be first is anyone's guess, and what you have to do to complete the task or straight up survive the trial is also unknown. Each portal lays a spell on the participants preventing them from speaking about their experiences." Zane said. "The portals also prevent anyone without a legitimate claim to the throne from competing."

"How does one get a legitimate claim?" I asked.

"Blood or power. You either need to descend from a prior Lucifer, or you need to have enough power running through your veins to challenge for the position."

I swallowed. We both knew which category I fell into. Would my lineage be enough? I felt like I was heading to a book club without having read the book. And I knew faking it and saying shit like, "this really resonated with me" wasn't going to cut it.

Zane kept talking as if I wasn't staring at the demon clothing and having a complete mental breakdown. "When you complete the first trial, a portal will appear to bring you back here."

I liked Zane. He said when I'd complete the trial, not if, and his confidence in my ability to survive the Inferno sent warmth through my body and eased some of the tension in my shoulders. "And then?"

"Eat, sleep, and repeat, until you successfully complete all six trials. Usually, the council runs a trial every morning with a small break in the middle between the third and fourth one. There is little downtime to heal, practice or learn about the next trial. It's intense. Like an inferno."

I stared at the black material in my hand and shoved my head through one of the holes. Nope. That was a hole for an arm. "Anything else? Anything specific about the actual trials?"

Zane cast a concerned look over his shoulder but thankfully continued. "The first trial stipulates no weapons, so this trial probably doesn't involve combat."

"Are they going to frisk us?" I asked. "Or is this like a prison where favored inmates get to sneak in shivs?"

Zane grunted and shook his head. He folded his

arms over his chest, making his massive biceps pop. "No one will have a weapon if weapons aren't allowed. The portals prevent it. But remember what I said last night, the Council of Six may be big on rules and fairness before you enter the portal, but once you step through those gates, there are no rules. Expect the unexpected. Expect treachery. Trust no one."

Lovely. I pulled on the rest of the shirt.

Something scratched on the other side of the door. Zane stepped forward and opened it, still keeping his back to me.

"Hey! I'm still changing here." I held the leather pants over my chest.

Chupey sauntered into the room, the handles of my duffle bag clenched between his teeth. After he passed Zane, he spat the handles out, dropping the bag at my feet. "You look ridiculous."

I dropped the pants, no longer caring that I stood in my underwear and a string shirt in front of Zane. "Chupey, buddy. Please tell me that bag is—"

"Full of your gear. Yes. And clean underwear."

"Underwear?" Zane raised both eyebrows.

"Yeah, humans are big on it for some reason," Chupey said.

I dropped down on my knees and hugged him, scratching behind his ears, and ignored his comment that implied demons all walked around commando.

Zane snorted. "He's not actually a dog you know."

"I know." I squeezed Chupey harder.

Chupey snuggled against my chest. "Don't listen to him. Familiars live for this shit. It's like crack."

I laughed and gave his neck some more pats and scratches before pulling away and straightening.

Zane looked at both of us as if we'd lost our minds. "I'll wait outside."

"Thank you."

After Zane stepped out, I quickly peeled off my clothes and redressed in something more comfortable and familiar. Chupey went through what to expect with the trials, and his information matched Zane's almost word for word—vague and not insightful. Apparently, no one really knew what to expect, thanks to the non-disclosure spells. That wasn't bad news for me. That meant I wouldn't be the only person clueless.

I opted to wear my black training shorts. They might be tight and short, but they allowed for movement. After throwing on my armor-like sports bra with the enforced straps and front zipper, I pulled one of my sporty tank tops over the bra.

Turning to Chupey, I placed a hand on my hip and asked, "How do I look?"

"Like a human."

I sputtered. I was human. Well, half human. "Is that such a bad thing?"

"It's a weakness and best not to flash it around like a neon sign."

I threw up my hands. "I don't know what to expect and I need to be comfortable and able to move freely without worrying about my clothes. This is what I know."

"I know."

"And you said I looked ridiculous in the demon top."

"You did."

"Chupey! You're not being helpful," I said. Picking up the strappy shirt thing, I pulled it over the black tank top. "There."

Chupey snorted.

"And I'm not wearing those boots." I pulled on white ankle socks and slipped my feet into my running shoes.

Chupey whined.

"I'd rather look human than stupid," I snapped.

Zane knocked on the door. "Times up. Get your ass out here."

I opened the door and Zane stepped back, eyes widening as he scanned my body.

"I don't want to hear it," I shot.

He snapped his mouth shut and nodded. "Fine. This way."

Zane held out his spear, and for the first time, I was able to get a good look at it. It was over seven feet in length and made of some sort of black metal. More importantly, the weapon had a gnarly spearhead. When the morning light streaming in from the windows hit the edge, it shone, betraying the sharpness.

I shuddered. Fully aware I had no weapon to carry into these trials and some demons may not want me to compete, I stayed between Zane and Chupey. They walked with relaxed demeanors and bantered back and forth, like two long time friends would, regardless of being Hell creatures or the deadly challenges awaiting me. I wanted to take their nonchalance as a compliment, that they believed I'd win the Inferno trials easily, but I wasn't feeling the same confidence. My nerves made nausea roll in my gut.

When we entered the throne room, I was faced with a dense crowd of demons of all shapes and sizes. The place was packed. Some had horns, some didn't. Some had long hair that fell down their backs in soft waves, some had locs, some had short hair and some had no hair at all. They had a variety of skin tones, some similar to those found in the mortal realm, some completely different and foreign, like blue and green. They were all fit. And they all wore strappy, leather contraptions and combat boots. I looked like a cream puff in comparison. And no one who knew me would ever think or dare to compare me to a pastry.

Chupey was right, I stood out and may as well carry a neon sign announcing my humanity.

"Whoa." I rocked back on my heels.

"The trials shall begin shortly," a loud male voice boomed over the crowd.

The conversations faltered and died as everyone turned toward the throne.

Six demons stood on the dais. The male who spoke had two sets of twisted horns protruding from his head, much like Zane. He wore a long flowing robe the same color as clotted arterial blood and his red-slit eyes flashed with intelligence.

"That's Malachi," Zane leaned down to whisper into my ear. "He'll officiate the first trial. Expect to use those brains of yours. Malachi likes riddles."

"Do you two hang out?"

"Hang out?" Zane waggled his eyebrows at me. "Yeah, sure. That's what we do."

The demon in question turned away and raised his hands, his robe falling back to reveal forearms corded with muscle. Magic flowed into the room, brushing over my skin.

I gasped. Something inside me rose up to answer the call. I clenched my hands, my nails digging into my palms.

Pain answered. I frowned and looked down. Blood dripped from my fists. Opening my palms revealed four small puncture wounds. My normally short nails had elongated into talons.

Talons.

Chupey bumped into my legs. "Better put those away."

"How?" I hissed.

"Relax."

Oh yeah, sure. Relax. Because that was a totally

natural response to have when faced with talons growing and demon portals.

I squeezed my eyes shut and took long, deep breaths. My fingers tingled and when I opened my eyes, I found my normal nails had returned.

"Why do I need to hide them? Didn't you already criticize me for looking too human?" I whispered to my familiar. "And it's not like anyone else is hiding their demon shit."

"You look human, act human, and insist on dressing human," Zane whispered. "May as well embrace it and let them assume you're weak like a human. It's not the approach I would've taken, but in hindsight, it might be for the best. Let them underestimate you."

Oh. That made sense. Unlike everything else. I still had so many questions, but one thing, in particular, kept bothering me. "I'm still pissed Ryker lied to me."

Chupey cocked his head. "What do you mean?"

"He said I had two weeks to present myself to the council. If I had listened to him, I would've missed this entirely."

"He didn't lie," Zane said.

"What?"

"He didn't lie," he repeated, only slower. "Until yesterday's announcement, you still had two weeks to claim your inheritance—sixty-six days and six hours after the time of your father's death."

"Then what changed? How'd they know to start

now? We'd just arrived when Chupey got the memo about the trials."

Zane and Chupey went quiet.

"Is there some sort of silent alarm? Did they know I was here and planned to claim the throne the second we stepped through the portal?"

"They didn't," Zane answered, mouth turned down.

"Then why'd they start the trials?"

"I told them to," a familiar voice cut in.

I whirled around in time to watch the crowd part for Ryker. Wearing boots, leather pants, and a shirt that exposed more than it hid, he stood out even in a room full of demons. Dark energy swirled around him and licked my skin.

"You told me you had no interest in the throne and I relayed the information to the council," he said. His gaze drifted from my face and his lips curled up. "I should've known you'd be a redhead."

I took an involuntary step back to get away from the enticing feel of his power. "What are you doing here?"

He cocked his head, his dark gaze flashing. "I could ask you the same thing, princess."

Princess? Really?

What a fucking piece of—

"You look a little flushed," Ryker said. "Not sleeping well?"

Memories of Dream Ryker spiraled up and if I

wasn't flushed before, I definitely blushed now. Heat spread across my face and down my neck.

"You need to stay out of my dreams, charmer."

His eyebrows rose and a slow smile spread across his face. "I have many skills, Sloane. Many. But controlling or projecting myself into someone else's dreams isn't one of them."

Fuck.

He leaned in. "Tell me...how was I?"

Right. Like this wasn't one-hundred percent embarrassing.

"You need to leave." I raised my hand and flicked it back and forth in a shooting motion. "You're stuffing up the place with your inflated ego."

His lips twisted into a condescending smirk. "I'm not going anywhere. You'll have to get used to me."

Yeah, I didn't like the sound of that at all. "Why's that?"

Zane stepped in. "Because, aside from you, Ryker is the top contender for the throne, and you'll have to travel with him to the trials."

CHAPTER TEN

"I'm not traveling with him." I shook my head, lips rounding as I ground my teeth. "I'm not going *anywhere* with him."

Maybe I sounded like a petulant child, but my reaction was justified considering what Ryker planned to do. What he'd always planned to do. I glared at him like I could somehow perform magic and kill him on the spot.

It would save me a lot of hassle in the end.

He'd manipulated me from the start. I'd reacted badly to the information about my father and the Inferno, and he made sure to run off and rat me out to the council right away. If I had hesitated for even a day, he would've had a clear path to the throne, and I would be heading straight to the grave.

Asshole.

I refused to give Ryker the satisfaction of backing

down, and like hell I'd go anywhere with him now. He'd touch me when my back was turned and use his powers on me. Maybe I could resist his magic like last time, maybe I couldn't, but he'd try to make me skip the Inferno and hand the crown over to him with a smile on my face.

Not happening.

"You're not going to have a choice. All eligible contestants must travel to the trials in a single group," Zane said.

"What?" I turned to him. "Why? Does Ryker need to hold his mommy's hand?"

Ryker chuckled somewhere behind me.

"It's to help deter cheating." Zane looked apologetic. He adjusted his grip on his spear, the point reaching higher than the horns on his head. I was grateful to have him with me, even if that spear probably wouldn't do shit against Ryker. Zane's sympathy meant I had someone else in my corner besides my familiar, who kinda had to have my back, considering we'd been together for ten years.

Several other demons stood together, and their gazes bore through me. The same thing I'd been trying to do, but way more effective. I could take a few notes from them. If I made it through these trials, I'd be their boss, which meant I not only needed to match their scathing expressions but do them better.

Ryker stepped up beside me and waved at a portal already called into existence. "Now, if you please."

"I *do* please, thank you," I muttered under my breath.

But I held back, watching the others despite the niggling desire to stride to the head of the group and show these jerks it wasn't just my bloodline that would help me win the title. It was me, personally, and all the crap I'd been through in my life.

Ryker didn't care about any of those things. He didn't care about me, period. We were both after the same thing. Why did he come to my apartment? Maybe it had nothing to do with feeling out my intentions to claim the title but to intimidate me into not trying at all.

Either way, Ryker, for his part, looked as happy about this situation as a kid facing a root canal. He crossed his arms over his chest and stared down Chupey with his lips zipped the way I'd wished they'd been before. A Chupacabra bumped into Ryker's leg before looking up at him adorably.

"Good luck, Ryk," a demon growled. He stepped up to punch Ryker in the shoulder.

Ryker pointed down at the familiar leaning into his leg. "You'll take care of her?"

The demon nodded. "Of course."

I blinked. Was this a...friend? And why did the idea of Ryker having friends seem so preposterous?

Right.

Because he was a dick.

Along with poor taste in friends, this demon had

long black hair with the scalp underneath shaved. Two black horns protruded from just behind his forehead and curled toward the back of his neck. He narrowed his piercing blue eyes on me and scowled, revealing white teeth and long fangs.

"Come on, Zi," the demon said.

The familiar whined but straightened from Ryker's leg to follow the demon through the crowd.

"Never pegged you as a family man." I studied my nails. "Why can't Zi go with you?"

"I don't want her to."

"Why?" I didn't understand it. Though Chupey couldn't accompany me to the actual trial, he could go through the throne room portal and travel to the trials with me. As long as Chupey was allowed, I wanted him with me. He knew more about what was going on; he was my anchor during the stormy seas. Just as he had been in the living realm for all those years. I needed him with me.

"She doesn't need to see what it means if I lose," Ryker said.

Oh.

Oh.

That was dark. Even for him. But I could respect the compassion he had for his familiar. I just didn't think he was capable of such an emotion at all.

"This is going to be interesting." Ryker's scoff shattered the millisecond of empathy for the guy. "When I told you about the tests before, you said you had no intention of trying to pass them. Yet here you are."

He watched me, his green eyes narrowed almost the same way as his friend's had moments ago. Was the demon a friend? Or was he a brother or a lover?

The room around us filled with anticipation the longer he held my gaze and I half-expected a small thundercloud to burst to life above his head.

"I changed my mind," I said.

"And you think you're going to win the Inferno? After repressing your power for twenty-five years? You'll be lucky to survive the first trial. You're obviously out of your fucking mind."

"Then I'm in good company," I told him. "Now stand aside and enjoy the show. Feel free to make yourself comfortable."

His attitude didn't discourage me as he most likely intended, nor did it foster a sense of dread, or doubt, or fear. Instead, he spurred me on. His comments fueled my fire.

"Death awaits you on the other side of that portal," he said in an undertone, loud enough for me to hear but no one else. "You should turn away now while you have the chance."

Little did he know, death awaited me everywhere. "I'm so touched you care."

"Is this a joke?" he asked.

"If it is, you're the punchline." I'd enjoy watching him break and falter. If he held his breath waiting for me to fail, then I'd watch him go down blue-faced, too. Either way, I'd be a winner.

Ryker scoffed again, towering over me like he could use his height to intimidate. Had he learned nothing while he'd watched me? I didn't intimidate easily.

"You have an inflated ego if you think you stand a chance against me," he said. "Or any of these other competitors. You're completely ignorant of this world and ways, and your laughable human outfit just proves it. You're powerless. You're weak. What are you going to do? Try to punch your way through the trials?"

"I'm not completely ignorant." I gave him a half-shrug. "I've been competing and kicking ass for years. So yeah, I think that plays to my advantage. This is just another match for me to win. And you can bet your sweet ass I'm going to win it."

I pushed my way in front of him, feeling him rolling his eyes at my back more than seeing it.

"Speaking of *ass,* you might be annoying, but I do enjoy watching you walk away," Ryker called out.

Was he hitting on me? It was starting to sound like it.

Better yet, why was my body responding to his piggish comments at all? My stomach was twisting into knots, and not in the way it should. Frankly, it was pissing me off.

"Keep your eyes to your fucking self," I muttered under my breath.

He caught up to me in a single stride.

"Have you ever thought about smiling more? You're—"

"Don't you fucking dare finish that sentence."

He was kidding, right? It was like he had a list of the top ten things never to say to a woman and he was just checking them off as he went to see when I'd snap.

When I glanced over and saw his victorious smile, I knew my assumption had been right. He was doing everything possible to get under my skin.

Asshole.

I couldn't let him get in my head and distract me. That was what he wanted, and I *knew* that. I had to just ignore him.

We were the last two to step through the portal to the trials. The magic washed over me as I stepped onto uneven ground. I tore my gaze away from Ryker and froze. The portal had taken me to a cliff edge on the side of a mountain. Six smaller portals stood ahead of me on the edge of the cliff, along with open sky and wilderness far, far below. The light breeze played with my red hair, carrying with it a faint blend of pine, ocean, and something slightly charred. I whirled around. The portal we'd stepped through pulsed along the side of the rock face that continued to rise up to the clouds. The only way off this platform was by portal or death.

"Why do you want a throne you know nothing about anyway?" Ryker pressed, distracting me from the sights. "Just because you think it's something you should do? You don't have the will. You lack the determination."

"Trust me, I've got the determination. I've got more determination in my finger dripping blood than you do in your entire body. You look like you haven't struggled for a thing in your whole damn life. I might be the daughter of the last Lucifer, but I sure as hell wasn't brought up with a silver spoon in my mouth." I kept my attention forward, Chupey gave me silent moral support, knocking into the side of my leg every few steps as though to remind me of his presence. I appreciated it more than he knew.

"And, honestly," I continued, apparently on a roll. "I don't have to answer to you."

"Actually, you should get used to answering my questions. When I'm the next Lucifer—"

Okay, the guy wasn't going to stop. I whirled on him and flipped him the finger. "Are you trying to piss me off?"

I didn't expect him to smile. "It looks like I already have."

And I'd walked right into it.

Like hell I'd give him the satisfaction of playing his little head games. Turning my nose up in the air to show him how much I didn't care, I strode off toward the others waiting for the first trial to start. They'd grouped together near the first of the portals, the one farthest to the left.

Apparently, Ryker didn't like being ignored. He

reached out and grabbed me by the arm, halting my movement. I had the choice of struggling against his hold or whirling around to face him once again. I chose the latter and jabbed my finger into his chest. "What's your problem?"

Our gazes met. Fire burned in his eyes, and he pressed his lips together. His stubborn expression probably mirrored mine, right down to the furrowed brow and teeth gnashing.

"You're infuriating," he ground out.

"Thank you. I do my best."

He took a step closer, crowding my space and taking up all the air. The size and breadth of him... damn. They didn't make men like this in the mortal realm. He was gorgeous. And I hated myself for the thought because he was also an asshole, and out to steal what was rightfully mine.

Not to mention the human table bit.

I wasn't sure I'd ever forgive him for that.

I glanced between his hand on my elbow and his face. "You want to let go of me now."

He stared down at me, anger simmering beneath the surface. I might understand his hatred toward me now, but why the hell did he also look...

No, wrong. Desire couldn't possibly flash in his gaze. I had to be mistaken.

"What is it about you?" Ryker spoke more to himself, probably not intending for me to hear or answer.

I lifted a brow, not wanting him to see the hurt. I already knew I didn't fit into this new world. I didn't need the fan-favorite to remind me about it every other question. My confidence could only carry me so far.

"I'm one of a kind," I replied.

A single tug brought me to his chest, my palms slapping hard pecs that might as well be carved of stone. Heat curled immediately in my core and shot out pleasantly to the rest of my limbs.

"Let go," I said.

Ryker didn't listen.

Once again, neither one of us wanted to back down. He refused to let go and I refused to make him. I needed to save the rest of my energy for this trial, especially considering how my last fight at the Underground went.

"Well?" I asked.

The demand, coupled with the searing eye contact, should have done the trick. Instead, Ryker tightened his hold on my elbow while the other hand snaked around my lower back in a vice grip.

"What are you going to do, Sloane?" he asked in a low rumble of sound. "Why don't you make me let you go? Show me what you've got."

Oh, I'd show him, all right. But not the way he expected.

Not the way I expected, either, because I lunged at him. Mouth first.

I rose on my tiptoes to capture those plump, delicious lips with my own, grinding against his steel body. Sliding my hands up to his neck to tangle my fingers in his hair, I kept him in place.

Once again, Ryker refused to back down.

And this time I was so glad for it.

He growled, his arms becoming a cage around me as his tongue darted out to tangle with my own. His dream kiss had been divine. This was even better. The heat inside of me ignited into a full inferno.

I wanted more.

I wanted everything.

His touch was like a drug, increasing in intensity with each lick.

He pushed away.

We scrambled back from each other and I panted, blinking at him. My chest heaved, hands curling at my sides to keep from touching him again.

But I wasn't done with him.

From the fire flicking in his emerald gaze and his scar visibly glowing red, he wasn't done with me either.

We lunged together in unison, his hand squeezing my ass to pull me tight to his body. On a mountain ledge, in front of everyone waiting for the trial to begin, we made out like two drunk college freshmen at a frat party. I was ready to jump and wrap my legs around his waist to relieve the ache inside of me, to hell with the audience. To hell with hating him.

A distant part of my mind remembered he

controlled people by touch. He was definitely touching me, but it wasn't his power that made me want him.

His kisses were passion and light. They were searing and possessive and what I'd been missing in this life. Our mutual dislike of each other didn't matter. Nothing else mattered because I lost myself in him.

Well, damn.

When we broke apart the second time, I didn't try to grab him again. Something about his body language changed from open and aggressive to just pure aggressive.

Any lingering desire fled as he visibly shut down.

"I'm going to beat you today, Sloane," he told me. "I'm going to beat you because you don't deserve the throne and I do."

I swiped a hand over my still pulsing lips. "That is a matter of personal opinion."

"No, it's not. My great-grandfather used to hold the title of Lucifer until your grandfather betrayed him and took the throne."

I winced at the harshness of his voice.

Ryker continued, his face pulled into a dark grimace. "When that happened, my entire family was cursed. Reduced to scrubs, the lowest of the low. I've hated your family since birth. I've hated everything your bloodline stands for because of what it cost me and mine."

Shoulders hunched, he stomped past me toward the portals.

"I didn't have anything to do with what happened to your family," I said when his shoulder brushed mine.

He paused, only a step or two past me. "I worked my way up because I'm a smooth talker, and I was able to become a guardian of the gates, monitoring travel in and out of the Underworld. Hell's butler, some called me. But it's not enough. I plan to take back what rightfully belongs to my family. Either get the fuck out of my way...or die."

The low timbre of a loud gong interrupted my plans to cut Ryker down a notch or two. Give up or die? Who did he think he was?

I shouldered past him and stood with the group of contending demons. Ryker followed, stopping close enough behind me to breathe down my neck.

Doing my best to ignore him, I straightened to try to peer over the demons in front of me. The Council of Six now stood in front of the first portal with the royal guards, including Zane, forming a line on each side with their spears pointed at the group.

Zane must've walked away sometime during my make-out session with the enemy. Our gazes met and his lips quirked. I'd hear about the whole kissing thing later.

If I survived.

"Trial one will now begin," Malachi announced, his deep voice shaking my nerves.

Silence fell over the crowd, interrupted occasionally by the rustle of dirt as feet shuffled. No one stepped toward the portals.

That was it? That was the only direction the grand Council of Six planned to provide? Yeah, Zane and Chupey gave me a crash course, but surely the council planned to elaborate.

I stared down the portal as if it would start blabbing all its secrets if I glared hard enough. Each portal sat on the edge of the cliff, making the act of stepping into one a brutal trust exercise.

"What happens if someone without a claim tries to go through the portal?" I asked no one in particular.

"They fall off the cliff," Ryker replied. He leaned down, his breath fanning my neck. "It's time to find out."

"Find out what?"

"Who's your daddy."

I shot him an annoyed look. "We already know who my daddy is." Was.

Fuck.

Maybe I should've taken more of Zane's advice. I pulled down on the tank top and string shirt combo and turned back to study the portals again. I had no other choice. I had to walk through the portal. Staying here meant death. Returning to the mortal realm meant death. The only option that provided a modicum of possible survival stood in front of me with that eerie buzzing energy and blue swirling air.

I had to walk through it alone.

Instead of joining me, Chupey held back. He'd already told me he couldn't come along for the first trial, but the distance between us still cut at my chest. I wanted my demon familiar beside me.

Somehow, I'd drifted closer and closer to the first portal, the crowd parting for me. Warmth spread through my chest as the dark blue energy called to me, whispered to me, enticed not with words, but a pull of power. I was meant to do this.

I belonged here.

This close to the portal, the heat of its magic licked my face. I peeked over the ledge of the cliff and gulped. The treetops below were so far down, the drop easily over three-hundred feet.

I wouldn't survive the fall. No one would.

"Hurry up, princess," Ryker growled.

I startled, not realizing he'd trailed so close behind me, step for step, like the demonic stalker he was.

"Back off," I hissed through clenched teeth. "You're more than welcome to go first."

"Actually, tradition states the heir of the last Lucifer gets the honor." Ryker's tone dropped, low and growly, it vibrated against my skin.

My lips tingled, remembering our kiss and wanting more.

I snarled until the feeling went away. Now was not the time to process whatever that was.

The crowd behind me began to growl and snap

obscenities. They might respect tradition, but they certainly didn't respect me.

Chupey yipped in encouragement. Or maybe he just wanted me to hurry up, too, so he could nap.

"You could step aside and abdicate your claim." Ryker stroked his chin.

"Or..." I reached back and hooked my arm around his. "I could take you with me."

Without another word, I stepped through the swirling blue magic of the portal and hauled Ryker with me.

CHAPTER ELEVEN

I landed face first in a foot of water. Sputtering, I flailed until I managed to grip the slippery surface and pushed my head out of the water.

A dark cavern greeted me, along with a string of Ryker's cursing.

Oh my, demon boy was pissed.

Getting my feet underneath me, I stood and tried to shake out as much water as possible. My sneakers were ruined.

"What the fuck?" Ryker snarled and stomped over to me, splashing water in his wake. "Too chicken shit to do the trial by yourself?"

"Why don't you go run and tell the council on me? You're good at that."

He grabbed the stringy part of my shirt, hoisted me off the ground, and slammed me against the cave wall. "What's your deal?"

His face was impossibly close. He seethed with anger, his magic vibrating along my skin. Our breath mingled as we glared at each other, panting.

What was my deal? No clue. I didn't want to be alone and, apparently, having my enemy with me was better than no one at all. What had come over me?

Apparently, Ryker wasn't the only one questioning my actions.

I offered an awkward, one-shoulder shrug from my pinned position. "I'm kind of just winging it."

Ryker cursed again and pushed away from me.

I fell back to the ground and scrambled to my feet to look around. We were in a small, dark cave. Small holes in the ceiling let in shards of silvery light and trickles of rain. Glowing blue algae or fungus of some sort covered one of the walls, but the dim light made it hard to discern details.

A large pillar rose up from the center of the cave to the enclosed roof and though the main portion of the cave was roughly circular, it had a few nooks and crannies along the outer edge. The floor wasn't an even surface, with ledges rising up from the water. It would make walking around difficult, the entire cave floor a giant tripping hazard.

Ryker now stood a few feet away, raking his hand through his black hair as he also surveyed the situation.

The cave shuddered and water poured in through the holes. The pool of water rose from ankle depth to mid-shin. I searched frantically for an exit.

My skin tingled, my hindsight blaring its alarms.

Yeah, thanks magic. I'm aware of the danger.

"How do we get out?" I asked.

Ryker didn't answer.

"Ryker?" I spun to find him patting down the walls.

Okay...maybe bringing the village idiot wasn't the best of my ideas.

"The trials test aspects of leadership," Ryker growled. "This one must be intelligence. We have to find the way out."

I blinked at him. The incoming water slowed down in volume, now trickling through the pore-like holes at the roof of the cave.

"Like an escape room?" I shivered and rubbed my bare arms.

"There's not going to be a neon exit sign, princess. Hurry the fuck up and start looking before the water covers any clues."

I jolted into action, getting on my hands and knees to pat the covered ground of the cave. My fingers brushed along something hard. I clutched the object and brought it up.

A knife. A sheathed dagger.

Ryker still patted along the walls, his boots sloshing the water and almost managing to drown out his string of curses. He had an impressive vocabulary.

I shoved the dagger into my tight shorts, the handle sticking out a little, and kept searching. My hands grew numb, and I finally gave up on the ground and started on scouring the little ledges, relying more on my hands than my sight.

"I found a torch," Ryker called out.

A silver band of light illuminated a small box on a ledge jutting out from the ground. I plucked it from the rough surface and held it up. "I found matches."

We turned to each other, and I met his gaze easily, even in the dark cave.

"We need to work together," I said.

"Agreed." He didn't appear too happy about that, and it most definitely wasn't just the shadows of the cave playing on the angles of his face.

He really did hate me. He hated the idea of me and who I was. It didn't matter that I had nothing to do with my grandfather taking the throne, nor the poor treatment of his family ever since.

The cave shuddered and more water poured in, running down the walls of the cave in little streams.

Without further hesitation, I lit the match and pressed it to the torch Ryker held out until the fire caught. The thing must've been covered in fuel because flames rose up quickly, flooding the cave with warm light.

Ryker watched me, unreadable emotions flashing through his gaze with each flick of firelight.

The water flow eased off again, leaving the level of the water at my knees. If we didn't work faster, we'd drown in here, all the clues buried beneath the water.

"Let's keep looking," he said.

I turned away and gasped. "The wall."

Visible in the torch's light, a picture of vertical bands of paint stared back at me—blue, blue, white, yellow, white. "It looks like a code."

"Let's search for anything of the same color," Ryker ordered.

We stumbled around looking for something, anything, with color instead of the slate gray of the cave. I stubbed my toe on a hidden ledge beneath the water and swore, stumbling into one of the nooks. I flung my hand out to catch myself, and my fingers brushed thin paper. With my heart beating so hard it threatened to punch its way free from my chest, I pulled myself upright and snatched the paper from the little ledge.

A note.

A string of weird symbols ran across the thin slip of aged parchment in a single line.

Perfect. A demonic note required for my survival that I couldn't read. I tucked it in my shorts and dropped my head back to...What? Scream? Pray for divine intervention?

It didn't matter.

Staring back at me were long spikes of rock jutting down from the shorter ceiling of the nook. Icicle-like in shape, the cascading light from the torch in Ryker's hand nearby illuminated their various colors.

My breath caught.

The stalactites were red, blue, yellow, and white. Three of those colors matched the paint on the wall. I reached out and tapped them in the same order as the paint on the wall—blue, blue, white, yellow, white.

Nothing happened.

Dammit.

I tried the reverse order.

Still nothing.

"Ryker," I yelled over my shoulder.

He stomped his way over. The cave shuddered again, and the cave filled to waist level and Ryker had to wade the rest of the way.

Panic threatened to seize my lungs, but I pushed the feeling away. We were onto something here. We just needed a little more time.

"We're running out of time," he said, as if hearing my thoughts.

I pointed at the stalactites.

He clamped his mouth shut and reached up to tap the weird formations.

"I tried that."

When he tapped out the same sequence, he tried the order in reverse.

"Tried that, too."

He growled when his attempt didn't yield any results.

"I wonder if we need to take them down. What if we need to move them somewhere else?"

He froze, his gaze flicking to the section of the cave he was just in.

"What did you find?"

He pressed his lips together.

"We're supposed to work together." I placed my hands on my hips...right over the hilt of the dagger and where I'd stuffed the secret message. The irony wasn't lost on me.

"There are holes in the wall." He reached up and ripped a blue stalactite from the nook and handed it to me. I took it and waited while he ripped the rest down, stacking them in my arms like firewood.

"Come on." He waded past me, and we moved to the section he'd last searched. Sure enough, five smooth holes lined the wall.

The cave rumbled again, more water flowing in. The water level rose to my chest and covered the holes in the wall.

"Hurry," I said.

Taking one stalactite at a time from my arms, Ryker shoved them in the holes while still holding the torch with one hand.

The stalactites made a clicking sound once fully inserted. When Ryker placed the last one in, the cave rumbled again. More violently, the whole cave shook, slapping water against the walls. The column formation in the middle of the room shuddered and broke apart. Large chunks of rock fell into the pool of cold water, splashing me and Ryker.

My heart lodged in my throat. Had we done it? Was the trial over?

After the water settled, and I swiped the water and hair from my face, I scanned the room. The center column had transformed into a stone staircase.

My heart pounded. This was it. Our way to freedom.

More water poured in, and I had to swim over to the bottom steps. Ryker pulled himself from the water first and turned toward me. He hesitated, his expression contorted.

Was he going to betray me? Push me into the water and hold me down?

He better not.

I hung onto the bottom step and peered up, my breath caught in my throat. He shook his head a little, turned and jogged up the steps.

He didn't do it. He could have. He thought about it. But he left me to save myself.

I breathed out a sigh of relief and pulled my cold, bedraggled body from the water to clamber up the stairs after him. When I reached the top, I found him frowning. The stairs led to the top of the column, but there was nothing there. No exit hatch, no magical portal. Just the same gray rock surface that made up the rest of the cave.

I wrapped my arms around my chest and shivered. How was it possible to be in Hell, in summer, and freezing? There was a joke in there somewhere, but I was too cold and miserable to figure it out.

"There's a message." Ryker knelt down and brushed the dirt and dust from the small platform at the top of the column. The same weird symbol-style writing stared back at us.

The paper in my shorts burned against my skin.

"What does it say?" I asked.

He shook his head. "It's in ancient demonic."

Not what I asked. "Can you read it?"

"Yes, but it makes no sense."

I peered over the side of the stairs, the water continued to rise. "Just share the information. We're either dying together or surviving together."

"It says to form a portal with a drop of blood and an incantation."

"Okay..." I said. "I used an incantation to get to the Underworld, won't that work?"

"No," he said.

"Why not?"

"I already tried to form a portal earlier. The trial must be blocking the magic. We have to use their incantation."

"Okay, so let's do it."

"It doesn't provide the incantation, just a hint."

Of course. I pulled the stretchy material of my shirt back, pulled out the paper and held it out for Ryker to read. Soaked with water it drooped between my pinched fingers.

"What is this?" he asked.

I waved the slip of paper at him when he didn't take it immediately. "Hopefully the incantation."

"That you just happened to remember you had in your possession. What happened to the whole ride-or-die shit?"

"I didn't trust you to keep your word, okay."

"I always keep my word." He snatched the paper from my hand and scowled. His lips peeled back from his teeth. "That distrust just killed us."

"What?"

"I can't read this."

"Of course, you can. It's the same crap that's written on the ground."

He held the slip up to reveal the wet paper. The ink had run, smearing the symbols.

"Oh."

"Yeah. Oh." He swore again and turned away. Shoulders tense, he ran his hand through his hair.

An invisible rope tightened around my chest. My lungs constricted. Breathing hurt. I'd inadvertently destroyed the cave incantation, or at least the answer to the clue. "Wait. What was the hint?"

"What?" Ryker's rough voice growled.

"The hint," I repeated.

"It makes no sense."

"I don't care. We still have a chance."

He shrugged. "Why do demons and ghouls hang out all the time?"

I laughed. I laughed and I laughed as a giddy feeling overwhelmed me.

Ryker turned to face me, a deep frown contorting his face.

With a silent thank you to Zane and his terrible, god-awful jokes, I pulled the dagger free from its sheath, slit open my palm and squeezed my hand shut. Blood dripped from my clenched fists onto the message on the stones. I pulled all my anger and frustration from my core, focusing on the same feeling I'd needed to use to get to the Underworld and spoke clearly. "Demons are a ghoul's best friend."

Nothing happened.

Ryker stared at me, his mouth dropped open. Even though I couldn't actually read his mind, I didn't need to. He thought I'd lost all my marbles.

"Do you think I need to say it in demon?"

"I can't believe I'm about to do this." He shook his head, clearly wishing to be anywhere but here, and stepped close. He clamped his hand over mine, opened his mouth, and a bunch of demonic words poured from his lips.

A portal snapped open a foot away from us and we finished the trial the same way we started it.

Together, with Ryker scowling.

CHAPTER TWELVE

The second I stepped into the throne room from the portal, Ryker dropped my hand and stalked off into the stunned crowd. His friend and the demon familiar broke off from the group and left as well, trailing in his wake. Everyone else stared at me, their stunned silence making me freeze on the spot.

"Girl!" Chupey bumped into my leg. "Well, done. I'm so proud of you."

I reached down and scratched his head, not taking my gaze off the waiting crowd.

"What's wrong?" Chupey asked.

"They're not exactly cheering," I whispered back.

"They're not booing either. Take this as a win." Chupey nudged my leg with his snout. "Come on, let's get you some food."

Food was always Chupey's answer for everything, even before I learned he was a talking demon familiar.

"Fine," I said, knowing this was more for him than me.

He led me through the still-silent crowd and down the hallway, turning corners and leading me toward the warm smell of fresh bread and herbs. Without a word, he pushed through double swinging doors that opened to a grand room with rows of tables and benches.

Demons of various shapes and sizes already sat at a few of the tables, hunched over bowls of steaming soup with bread clutched in their hands.

"Is this some sort of demon cafeteria?" I peered around the room and took in the wooden beams and stark decor. Who paid for all this? How did the economy in the Underworld work? And if I won the throne, would I be expected to run all this shit right away, or was there some sort of apprenticeship program?

"Just sit," Chupey growled.

I must've been more tired than I thought, which said a lot. I did as ordered and plunked my ass down on a solid wooden bench and waited for Chupey while my mind continued to spiral.

Somehow Chupey got food in front of my face, but I barely registered what I shoved in my mouth. I kept coming back to the end of the first trial. If I hadn't pulled Ryker into my trial with me, I would've died. I would be drowning right now because I didn't know how to speak demon.

I glanced up and my gaze snagged on another demon with blue skin. The other demons around him chatted, argued, and laughed, but not this one. This demon, with ribbed black horns that looked like they could rip the flesh from my bones, sat a few tables away from me and glared as if he imagined my gruesome death.

Lovely, but honestly, right now, I didn't care. He could stand in line.

Stomaching as much food as possible without throwing up, I pushed the half-finished bowl away from me and left the demonic dining area and the angry demon behind. I just wanted to sleep.

No, that wasn't quite right. I wanted to smash the demon responsible for that trial and then sleep for a thousand years.

I stomped down the hallway, Chupey quick on my heels. My wet sneakers slapped against the tile floor, and I left a trail of dirty cave water in my wake. The gold-plated frames surrounding painted portraits of long-dead rulers blurred by me as red stained my vision.

"They're trying to kill me," I snarled.

"Mobius?"

I faltered, my feet missing a step. "Who's Mobius?"

"The asshole who glared at you while you ate."

"The blue guy?"

"Yeah, him. He's from Malachi's domain and yes, he very much wants you dead. He's also competing in the Inferno. He came out of the portal after you, but he couldn't have been that far behind because he arrived in the dining hall while I was getting you food. He didn't enter the Inferno by blood, so it means he's powerful. Watch out for him."

"I figured from his glare alone that he wants me dead. But I wasn't talking about him."

"Who, then?"

"The organizers," I said. "The council."

Chupey lunged forward to block my path. I skidded to a halt, the only option other than bulldozing over him.

"Why do you say that?" he asked.

I opened my mouth to speak, but the words wouldn't fall out. I swallowed and tried to tell him about the trial again. Nothing.

The spell of the portals prevented me from sharing details about the trials.

I took a deep breath and tried again. "I can't speak demon."

There. I said something without violating the portal's stupid magic restrictions, and Chupey could fill in the blanks.

"Sloane, everyone can speak demon. It's in your blood."

"I think I'd know if I could spit out a different language." I stomped past him, careful not to knock him over, and turned the corner. "I can barely speak English sometimes."

Zane and Ryker stood outside the door to my room and broke off what looked like an intense staring match to turn toward me. I stopped abruptly and Chupey ran into the back of my legs. My knees buckled.

I stumbled forward, my face heating.

Chupey coughed and slunk around me without an apology. Traitor.

Ryker leaned on the wall, one leg bent. He must've gone straight to his room and showered. Water still dripped from his hair, but he wore fresh clothes and didn't look like he'd just stepped out of a flooding death trap like I did.

Though he politely refrained from saying anything about my near face-plant, I wasn't ready to deal with him. I turned away from my competitor to face my other visitor.

Zane pressed his lips together, but the corners lifted up as he fought a laugh. He held a green bottle with dark liquid inside, wearing a skintight leather bodysuit that should've looked cheap or scandalous but somehow suited him. There's no way he would blend in the mortal realm.

"Please tell me that's alcohol." I nodded at the bottle.

He lifted it and waggled his eyebrows. "Absolutely."

"Perfect," I said. "You can stay."

Ryker's scowl deepened and he crossed his arms over his impressive chest.

I finally turned to him. "What are you doing here?"

He pushed off the wall and let his arms fall to his side. "I came to discuss your many shortcomings today."

My scalp prickled. If it weren't for me, he'd have died in that escape room.

And if it weren't for him, I would've died as well.

Bastard.

"My coming is none of your business, whether it's short or otherwise."

He smirked and stalked down the hallway toward me. Stopping short of touching, proving he had better control than my own familiar, he leaned down close, his minty fresh breath fanning my ear and neck. "Get Chupey to teach you how to embrace the demon."

"You really need to keep your kinks to yourself."

He huffed out something between a laugh and a chuckle, shook his head, and walked away.

"Why would you help me?" I spun to yell at his back. "I thought you were trying to win the throne?"

"I am." He spoke without turning, still walking away from me.

I frowned. That made no sense, unless his suggestion would somehow sabotage my chances.

He turned then, showing me his flashing gaze and smug smile. "I will win, Sloane. And when I do, we'll revisit this little conversation about *coming*. But winning is not nearly as rewarding if the fight isn't fair. Fix it."

He didn't feel the need to elaborate because the next thing he did was turn the corner and disappear from view, the sound of his footsteps fading away the only noise in the hallway.

I stood there, gaping at the empty hallway until I remembered to close my mouth.

"Come on!" Zane called out behind me. "Let's get drunk."

I shook my head and turned to find Chupey and Zane watching me expectantly.

"Who knows," Zane added. "Feed me enough shots and I might let you try to embrace this demon." He blew me a kiss.

I snorted, pushed thoughts of Ryker away, and walked back toward my room. Zane slung his arm over my shoulders and squeezed.

"So...embracing my demon. Please tell me there's not some sort of blood sacrifice required."

Zane snorted, releasing me so I could step forward and unlock the door. Swinging it open, I walked inside my personal paradise. Everything exactly where I left it, this place had quickly begun to feel like a home.

Home.

My mind instantly went to my other home—the

apartment in Braton. It seemed like I left years ago instead of yesterday.

Luckily, with the meager balance in my checking account and my line of credit, I had enough to cover the next couple of months of rent, but if I lingered too long, I'd have nothing to return to. I had bet all my savings on the fight, and had no job prospects.

Then again, if I didn't win the throne, I wouldn't need to provide for myself for much longer anyway. Wasn't that a pleasant thought?

How was Becca doing?

Did she end up coming over to visit last night after her date? Probably not. God, I hoped not. I also hoped I had a chance to smooth things over between the two of us and show her I could be a better friend.

I glanced around my current room as Zane and Chupey pushed past me and made themselves comfortable. Chupey threw himself down on the plush rug beside the bed and Zane hopped up to sit on the mattress.

"Why don't we start with what you already know," Zane suggested.

"Well, that's easy. I know a fuckton of nothing."

"Fuckton?" Zane tilted his head. "Is that a word?"

"It's a word."

"Doubtful." He uncorked the bottle and looked around, presumably for some cups.

I kicked the door shut behind me, took three steps to reach him and snatched the bottle from his hands.

He gaped at me as I placed the bottle to my lips and drank.

Cold liquid burned a path down my throat to warm my belly. It was like some raunchy mix between cinnamon whiskey and an herbal liqueur. It was absolutely disgusting and wonderful at the same time. I took another swig before holding it out for Zane.

He smirked and took it back.

"Don't tell me you have a thing about germs."

"Not at all, just wondering how to warn you about the potency of this stuff," he said. "Or whether I want to just watch what happens."

Chupey snorted. "Did you see her face? Of course, she knows."

Zane shrugged and tilted the bottle back, chugging a few mouthfuls of the demon brew. "Okay, back to what you know or you don't know."

"Chupey said some gibberish last night, but it made little sense at the time, and I was on information overload. I don't think my brain was ready to hear it then."

"And now?" Zane asked. "Is your brain ready?"

"Probably not, but it's readier than it was last night. So, you're up. Time to spill the tea. Maybe start at the beginning," I said, waving my hands around like that somehow represented going back in time.

Zane nodded. "The souls of the dead fuel the magic that demons access and use. Once the soul is essentially used up, they can be reborn. No soul is created or destroyed in the process, however, the more powerful the soul, the more power they provide us in the Underworld and the longer their soul spends fueling demons."

"Basically, what I already told you yesterday," Chupey huffed.

I patted his head.

My demon familiar arched into the contact and his tongue rolled out the side of his mouth.

Zane looked torn between disgust and amusement.

"Chupey did tell me something similar. So, souls are fuel?"

"Good and evil have no bearing on any of it. Souls are souls. Magic is magic. Power is power."

I blinked at him.

Zane cleared his throat. "But yeah. Souls are fuel."

"I'm not sure what to think about that," I said. I hadn't had a chance to really digest the information the first time I'd heard it, but a second time around the information made the wheels in my mind clank around a little bit.

"Then don't think of it at all," Zane replied. "Demons are just supernatural beings who live in another realm and wield magic. Simple."

"Simple?" Yeah, somehow I doubted that any of this was simple.

"Or..." Chupey perked up from the rug near my feet. "Think of the magic as a flow of energy, much like a flow of water. You need to find a way to access that stream. The ability resides within you. It's your own mortal soul that is most likely interfering."

"I've got mortal blockage?" I frowned and eyed the bottle in Zane's hand. He wordlessly handed it over.

"We have a lot of work to do," Zane said.

And, unfortunately, that wasn't an exaggeration.

CHAPTER THIRTEEN

I stared at the portal to the second trial, ignored the wailing sirens of my premonition magic, and waited for the pain medication to kick in. My head pounded and my vision wavered. Getting drunk last night hadn't been my best decision, but I'd been known to make worse choices.

The alcohol let me relax and helped me sense this weird tingle that Chupey assured me was my demon magic. It felt similar to the premonition magic I embraced in the cage and the anger I grabbed onto when I formed the portal to bring me to Hell, so once I recognized the similarity, reaching for it became easier and easier.

And I got drunker and drunker.

Miraculously, I only punched Zane once for making fun of me for tongue wrestling with Ryker before the first trial.

I met this morning with a headache and upset stomach, my mind so fuzzy, I hadn't put up an argument when Chupey and Zane chose my outfit for today.

So now I stood in front of the golden archway for the second trial in my tight shorts, layers of tank tops, and leather boots. At least I'd managed to braid my hair away from my face, the long red plaits falling down my back.

My image in the mirror still shocked me. In the light, my red hair almost had a pinkish tone and when I gripped my demonic magic, my eyes flickered as if they contained live fire. But at least I still looked like me. Mostly. I hadn't sprouted horns like most of the demons in the Underworld.

The crowd of contending demons had thinned out considerably. Apparently, a ton of demons didn't even make it through the portal, and only half of those who did managed to return. Of those survivors, a number of demons decided not to return for the second trial. Instead of a throne room packed with competition, only about a quarter remained.

Unfortunately, Mobius was one of them. He stood a few feet away, murder still evident in his red gaze.

I blew him a kiss.

"Rough night?" Ryker stepped up to stand beside me. He kept his gaze forward, studying the second portal. He wore leather pants and a matching studded vest that looked more like armor than a shirt.

"Fuck you."

"Say that again." He leaned closer. "I like how it sounds."

A shiver spread over my body, not from fear, but anticipation. God, I hated him. And I hated myself, too. "Why do you have to be such a dick?"

"Demon, remember?"

The magic for portal number two snapped into existence and a swirl of red filled the space inside the golden archway. A large demon with claw-like hands and flaming red eyes stood beside the portal. He didn't speak. Instead, a slow smile spread across his face.

I raised my eyebrows. The last portal had been blue and involved water. Lots of water. So much water, I had a lovely nightmare about it. If this one was red, what would it mean? Fire?

"Ifrit," Ryker noted. "Demon of the dead."

"What does that mean?"

"Failure will be painful."

Yeah, I didn't like the sound of that.

"Let's go." Ryker nodded toward the portal. "But you're on your own this time."

Ignoring Ifrit's creepy grin, I shouldered past Ryker and, without hesitation, marched through the portal.

I fell flat on my face, my forehead smacking against solid rock. Heat singed my hair and smothered my body. I pushed up from the rough surface and froze. Mere inches away from my face, magma bubbled and popped. Droplets of red, viscous liquid plopped down on the rocks and solidified.

If I had landed even slightly more forward, if I had sucked just a little more at walking through portals, my head would be melted in magma right now.

Shuffling away from the edge, I stood up and brushed the loose dirt from my shorts and legs. I stood on a rocky platform in some sort of valley. A sheer rock face rose up all around me while steam lifted off the burbling magma and made the air thick with heat. I was in some sort of a narrow ravine.

Sweat already dripped from my face and ran down my arms and legs.

Hah! I bet Ryker was melting in his warrior outfit.

I scanned the area and found him smirking at me from another platform a few feet away. The other contestants stood on similar platforms, positioned in a semi-circle in the magma, their expressions more hostile than Ryker's.

What in the fresh hell was this? They all faced the same direction. Little protrusions of rocks jutted out of the magma. Ropes hung down from thick wooden beams that ran overhead. Across the liquid death, a golden archway awaited. Presumably, that was the exit, but a whole lot of nope stood in my way.

This looked like a cross between a game where the floor was lava and a ninja training course. Demons might be responsible for this trial, but they obviously followed reality television from the mortal realm.

Motherfucker.

The ground I stood on rumbled and shook beneath my feet. Magma sloshed along the edges. *Yeah, I'm not hanging around for this shit.*

I leapt forward onto the next rock. It shuddered under my weight. My heartbeat thudded, the pumping in my veins so loud it consumed my hearing.

Behind me, the magma engulfed the platform I had stood on moments ago.

Ryker and the others had also moved forward, many were ahead, all moving toward what looked like a large common platform.

Yeah, that looked like a death trap waiting to happen. Straightening on my little perch, I scanned the layout. If I went around the large platform, I could still make it to the exit portal. Some of the rocks were spaced too far apart, but I could make it if I used the ropes.

Biting my lip, I let my mind work through the possibilities. I didn't want to die today, and this test wasn't really about intelligence, so much as physical stamina and if those rope ladders were any inclination, strength.

Gritting my teeth, I moved. Instead of heading to the center like everyone else, I made my way around the side. My muscles burned as I jumped from rock to rock, each leap longer until I made it to the last one before the ropes.

Cries and screams echoed along the ravine. The

others had reached the central platform and fights had broken out.

One of the white horned demons shoved another demon, one with small black scales, over the edge. The scaly demon screeched in pain, quickly engulfed by the magma.

Before the white horned demon could revel in her victory, another demon drove his long, spike-like talons into her back.

I swallowed, my heart threatening to punch free of my ribcage.

"Are you going to move?" A familiar deep voice spoke behind me.

My footing slipped. I flung my arms out, wind-milling in the air. I bent my legs and dropped into a crouch, my hand snagging onto the rock. I gripped it, hard, the jagged surface digging into my fingertips.

"That was close," Ryker said.

I cursed and whipped my head around to glare at him. "It was close because you scared the crap out of me."

He perched on the rock formation behind me, poised to leap onto my rock. "Would you prefer me to push you off the ledge like our comrades?" he asked.

I snorted and turned back to study the next hurdle. I needed to reach the rope, but it dangled over the bubbling magma. I could run and jump for it, but if I missed...

Game over.

"I have a suggestion," Ryker called out.

"If it's anything about my ass or your view, you keep it to yourself." I swiped at the sweat dripping down my face.

"It wasn't, but now that you mention it..."

I gripped the rock harder and glared at him over my shoulder.

He still crouched low, keeping his weight evenly distributed over the smaller rock formation.

"Look. There's enough room on your rock for both of us. Let me anchor you so you can reach out and grab the first rope. Once you're on, you can swing to the next rock, and I'll get the rope once it swings back this way."

I narrowed my eyes. "Why would you help me?"

"It's mutually beneficial. I don't feel like dying in magma soup today." He sighed and straightened from his crouch. "Look, I'm more vulnerable in this situation than you. If you wanted, you could push me off your rock the moment I jump over, or you could damage the final rope so I can't escape."

I tapped my chin as if I'd ever consider sabotaging someone like that. "How do you know I won't?"

"You're half human."

"Hardly grounds to claim moral superiority." *Has he seen humans lately?*

"But it's true for you."

Gah. He was right. "How do I know you won't

drop me in the magma instead of helping me?" He couldn't boast the same mortal morals like me, after all.

"Simple."

I waited.

"I need you to get the rope. You can't trust me to look out for you, but you can trust I'll look out for myself, and you're my ticket out of here."

"Fine."

He waved his hand at me, and I stepped over to the side. If he misjudged the jump, he could knock us both over into the magma soup.

My heart thudded, hard and painful. Maybe this wasn't such a good idea. Maybe I should just make a jump for the rope and hope I wouldn't miss and my sweaty hands wouldn't slip.

Before I had a chance to stop him, Ryker leapt from his perch and landed softly beside me with the grace of a fucking ballet dancer.

I scowled. He made that look entirely too easy.

"Okay, princess. You're up."

I let go of my perch and turned toward the dangling rope. It had a thick knot at the bottom. As long as I didn't miss the rope entirely or somehow slip completely off, my feet could rest on the knot and prevent me from falling into the skin-boiling magma.

"Just...back your ass up." Ryker opened his arms.

Instead of ripping into him, I did exactly as he directed. I was too hot and completely done with this trial already to fight or call him on his suggestive bullshit.

His hands came down on both sides of me, gripping my hips. His fingers dug in as I leaned forward.

My fingertips brushed the rough material of the rope. So close. Almost there. I leaned forward even more.

Ryker grunted behind me. His hands slipped a little and I shot forward. Not enough. The rope danced out of the way.

"Pull me back."

Without argument, he did, bringing me close into the heat of his body. My insides were already getting boiled in this heat. I didn't need—or want—the kind of warmth Ryker offered. My head swam. I needed water and space and about two more inches of arm.

"It's not enough," I said. "Do you think you can hold onto my hand without slipping? I'm a sweating mess, but I think I can get it if I reach for it sideways."

"I won't let you go," he growled.

I wiped my sweaty palms on my shorts and held my left hand out to Ryker.

He gripped my wrist, his entire hand encircled my arm. I held onto his forearm as best I could and leaned over the bubbling magma.

The steam rose and stung my eyes. Sweat dripped from my face and arms. I strained forward over the bubbling magma, and my hand closed around the rope.

With my breath caught in my lungs, I pulled the rope close. Finally.

"My grip," Ryker snarled.

My arm was slipping through his hands, and he grabbed for it with the other. His balance off, he lurched forward.

Time froze as he pitched forward toward me.

"Let go," I shouted.

His eyebrows shot up. His eyes widened.

"Let go!"

He did and I flew forward, clinging to the rope. I sailed through the steamy air until the momentum changed and I swung back.

Ryker had thrown himself to the ground to avoid the fiery death and he scrambled to his feet by the time I swung back to the rock.

"Need a push?" His smirk was back as if he hadn't almost died a second ago. As if we both hadn't risked our lives.

I squeezed the rope with both hands and legs, my feet securely anchored on the knot, and nodded.

Ryker placed his hands on my butt and thigh and pushed, sending me toward the next rope. With a shaky hand, I reached out, grabbed the next rope, and hopped over. Once I got my feet on the new knot, I released the first rope and watched it swing back to where Ryker waited.

We sailed over the magma, rope to rope, while the

other competitors continued to battle on the central rock, oblivious to the disappearing rock formations and the rising magma around them.

Mobius was there, stabbing demons with his horns and talons and shoving them over the edge. He roared and our gazes met. In that moment, I knew, if I had been on that central platform, I would be dead. I might've learned how to connect with my magic, but Mobius was a boss for a level I hadn't reached yet.

My arms burned. My lungs screamed. Sweat poured from my skin. I needed to make a final leap onto the platform with the portal.

Without overthinking it, I released the rope and sailed through the air. My body crashed onto the smooth rocky surface.

I made it.

I fucking made it.

I hopped to my feet in time to watch Ryker leap from the final rope. He sailed through the air and landed on his feet right at the edge of the platform.

He waved his arms, trying to fall forward, but his balance pitched him backward.

He wasn't going to make it.

I lunged forward, grabbed the leather vest, and pulled, sinking my weight back. We toppled over, crashing to the ground.

Ryker's body slammed into mine, knocking the air from my lungs. We laid like that for a stunned moment.

The wind had been knocked out of me, but Ryker's reasons for keeping me pinned under his weight were more questionable.

"You're welcome," I wheezed. "You can get off me now."

He propped himself up, his face impossibly close to mine, our bodies scandalously positioned, and glared at me. "What the fuck, Sloane?"

I shoved at him, and he slowly stood up. Without looking, he held his hand out to help me up. I ignored it and pulled my tired feet under me to get up on my own. I turned away from Ryker and stepped through the portal.

Magic tingled along my skin, and the cool air greeting me on the other side was the most fantastic sensation I'd ever felt. For the first time since this morning, my hindsight stopped sending tingles all over my body.

Ryker followed me through the portal, close on my heels. He reached out, gripped my arm, and spun me around.

I snapped my eyes open and glared. God, I hated him. What was his problem? I shook my arm free and wiped my sweaty hair from my face.

"Why would you save me?" he growled. "I thought you wanted the throne."

"No, I need the throne," I said. "But I don't want to sacrifice everything I am and stand for to get it."

His gaze darkened and he stepped impossibly close. The unique scent of vetiver and violence that always seemed to cling to his skin wove around me. "What do you mean, you *need* it?"

"Since you're always so quick to point out my mixed ancestry, I'm surprised you don't already know."

He frowned, his two dark brows sloping downward almost comically.

"I'll die without it, okay?"

With a snap, he straightened, blanking his expression. "Who cursed you?"

His words were soft, quiet, almost gentle—if anything about Ryker could ever be described in such a way. But his tone didn't match the anger and promise flashing in his gaze. Why did I get the feeling he planned to hunt down and hurt anyone I named?

I stepped back involuntarily. His fingers dug into my arms and held me in place.

"Who, Sloane?"

"My mom and dad, I guess," I answered. There was no harm in naming them. Ryker couldn't hurt them, wherever they were. "If I don't embrace my demon nature fully and take the throne, it will destroy my human side and kill me."

"You don't—" Ryker snapped his mouth shut. He blinked at me long enough for me to consider using force to free myself from this awkwardness. With a silent shake of his head, he relaxed his hold on my arm, and a slow smile tugged at his lips. "You better buckle up and prepare yourself then. I don't plan to let your sob story sway me from taking what's mine."

"It's not a sob story. It's the truth."

"If you say so."

CHAPTER FOURTEEN

I slipped away from the dining hall of Hell, leaving Chupey to his feast. After the adrenaline rush left me from the hot mess trial, and the sweat dried to leave my skin cold and clammy, my limbs grew heavy and my eyelids heavier.

Nap time.

My footsteps echoed down the empty hall illuminated by torches. My familiar was always most content with his face shoved in a dish of food, and it seemed selfish to drag him away just because I didn't have much of an appetite. I'd forced the food past my lips because I knew the importance of fueling the body, but after I stomached the bare minimum, I wanted to leave. My mind kept replaying the last trial. Once again, I'd survived. I'd passed. I hadn't sucked. But once again, my accomplishment dimmed in the shadow cast by this nasty fact I couldn't deny. I'd survived because of Ryker.

Sure, I'd saved his ass, too, but I'd...needed...him. I'd never needed someone before. And the idea didn't sit well with me. I hated this. I hated him. What kind of ruler did I hope to become if I couldn't survive on my own? If I needed *him*?

And what had Ryker planned to say when I told him about my diagnosis? He'd started to say one thing and then stopped, abruptly saying something else. Did he know something? What could he know that Chupey and Zane didn't?

My hindsight prickled and I rubbed my neck trying to smooth the hair down.

"Mortal," a deep voice growled behind me.

I spun around to find the giant blue bastard lurking in the hallway. Shirtless, his rippling muscles glistened under the flickering firelight. Thankfully, he wore a sort of leotard loincloth with fur to cover his man bits, but the guy was pretty much naked, and looked like the demons from nightmares. His hulking body took up almost the entire width of the hallway, and he easily stood over seven feet tall. Dried blood from his victims coated his forearms and flaked off his horns.

"Mobius." I dipped my chin.

His eyes widened and he stalked forward.

That's right, big boy. I know your name.

"You and I have some things to...*discuss*." His red gaze remained focused on me, cold and detached.

A shiver ran up my spine and a memory of him locking eyes with me during the trials spiraled up in my mind. He'd wanted me dead then, and from the curl of his thin lips and clenched hands, he wanted me dead now.

"I have nothing to say to you, smurf." I crossed my arms over my chest. "You'll have to wait until the next trial to hash out your grievances. Attacking competitors in between trials is against the rules."

Instead of stopping or appearing deterred by my words at all, he closed the distance between us, stopping only a couple of feet away. "You silly, vapid thing. You seem so confident standing here in this empty hallway spouting rules like they'll protect you."

"But...the rules..." I unfolded my arms, seeing the threat even if I didn't quite understand it.

"They discourage cheating between the trials." He leaned in. "But it's not forbidden, and if a bitch dies in an empty hallway, and no one's around to see it, who's to say it was murder? Who's to even look for someone to blame?"

A chill ran along my skin. I tried to peer over his shoulders, but they blocked out my view of the hallway. If I screamed, Chupey wouldn't reach me from the dining room in time and what exactly could he do? Chupey might die trying to protect me and that was the last thing I wanted. My best chance at survival was to turn and run for my room.

My hindsight screeched at me, and I shifted to the side, narrowly avoiding a dagger to my middle.

Mobius snarled and threw his head to the side. His horn smashed into my face. Pain exploded in my skull, and I reeled backward. My head rang.

I'd been hit before, but not like that.

Blinking rapidly, I ducked under Mobius' swinging backfist. Quickly, I jabbed out, swiveling my hips and throwing my weight behind the strike to his kidneys. One. Two.

Mobius growled and lashed out with his dagger. I jumped back, narrowly missing the tip. He might have a weapon. He might have a lot of muscles and power. But I was faster.

Darting in again, I struck at his throat.

Mobius's eyes widened and he choked. His meaty hand flew up to his throat as he gasped for air. His other hand punched out, trying to drive the dagger into my stomach.

Bastard.

Anger welled up inside me and I let it out. A wave of magic blasted from me like a shockwave.

Mobius stood frozen, stunned.

Not one to show mercy, I took the opportunity to kick him in the balls as hard as I could. Most men expected women to attack their genitals first, easily deflecting an attack. The key was to wait. The key was to strike them somewhere else, distracting them from my true intent, and then use a well-placed kick or knee to the nads as a finishing move.

My magical outburst faded away. Mobius groaned and keeled over.

I stood a foot away and watched this vile creature roll around on the ground. He'd planned to kill me, to gut me in the hallway, and now he lay on the floor choking and holding his junk. I hoped I popped a testicle.

He still grasped his dagger tightly in one hand. Part of me wanted to stick around, take a chance, and try to get the weapon from him. If I killed him now, he couldn't come after me later.

But the other part of me knew that wasn't the smart play to make. Whatever that magical blast thingy was, I had no way of knowing whether I could duplicate it and I didn't want to get stabbed trying to make a grab for a dagger.

Mobius wouldn't die by my hand tonight.

I made the smart move, spun on my heel, and ran to my room. My heartbeat thudded in my ears and my breath rasped through my lips, burning my chest.

When I rounded the last corner before my doorway, I skidded to a stop.

Ryker waited outside my room. He leaned on the door, arms folded, one leg propped up against the wood. He wasn't alone.

His friend stood across from him in the hall in

almost the exact same position, and the demon dog lay curled at Ryker's feet.

Ryker lifted his head at my approach and pushed off the door. The friend kept his position, only turning his head, while the familiar merely popped one eye open.

"Wh...what are you doing here?" I asked.

Instead of answering, Ryker stalked toward me, his green eyes flashing.

"I really don't have the energy for you to try to kill me in the hallway right now," I said, only partly joking. If Mobius felt bold and confident enough to attack me, that meant anyone could, and would, given the opportunity. Even Ryker.

Ryker snapped his hand out and jerked my chin up. His gaze flashed as he glared at my face under the flickering candlelight. When he finally spoke, his voice came out as a low growl. "Who hurt you?"

I jerked my chin out of his grasp and looked away. "It doesn't matter."

"The fuck it doesn't," he growled. "Who. Fucking. Hurt. You?"

The other two had moved, leaving their positions outside my door to stand behind Ryker and crowd my space.

"Who are your friends?" I nodded over Ryker's shoulder to the demon with black, half-shaven hair.

"Don't look at Slade. Look at me, Sloane. I'm your biggest problem right now," Ryker pinned that piercing green gaze on me. Reaching out, he ran his thumb over my lip. Pain shot through my mouth. He pulled his hand away, and my blood decorated his finger.

Well, crap. The blue bastard had cut me with that head strike.

Still keeping his gaze locked on mine, Ryker brought his thumb to his mouth and wrapped his lips around it, sucking off my blood.

That...

That was...

Did I like that?

The warmth flooding my core said yes, but my mind said hell no, he didn't just do that. "You have issues."

He withdrew his thumb and his lips twitched. "You have no idea."

My mouth dropped open. This would be the perfect opportunity to say something witty or scathing, or something to get rid of him so I could enjoy the safety of my own room, but instead, I kept replaying the image of him sucking his thumb in my head. Because apparently, I had issues too.

"It's against the rules to attack a competitor between trials," Ryker said, his voice dangerously low.

"No. It's discouraged." I folded my arms over my chest. *But it's not forbidden, and if a bitch dies in an empty hallway, and no one's around to see it, who's to say it was murder?* I dropped my voice, imitating Mobius and his dickish tone.

Ryker narrowed his eyes at me. As suddenly as he'd invaded my space and made heat stir within me, he straightened and backed away. "Make sure you lock your door behind you."

Apparently, the inquisition was over. That was easy. "Wait. What's the catch?"

Ryker jerked his head at his companions and brushed past me. "No catch, princess. Goodnight."

I watched him leave with Slade and the demon familiar, and a sense of trepidation settled over me. I wanted to run after him and ask what he was up to. I hadn't given him Mobius's name, but his abrupt departure and purposeful walk said a lot more than he did.

To my shame, though, I didn't run after him. I didn't find a weapon to finish my business with Mobius, either. Instead, I did exactly as Ryker suggested. After I locked my door, I cleaned up and let exhaustion take over.

CHAPTER FIFTEEN

Zane held up the soft tortilla wrap and smacked me across the face.

I jerked back and hissed. "What the hell, Zane?"

Without hesitation, he raised the tortilla and smacked me again. With my hands bound behind my back, I stood beside Chupey in the warm kitchen, unsure what I was doing here, let alone why this demon was hitting me with the worst part of a taco.

Zane had lured me here with promises of unlocking my powers. I'd readily agreed because anything was better than sitting around in my room, nervously awaiting for the council to announce the start of the next trial. I'd expected an educational, much welcome distraction to ease my nerves.

I didn't expect Zane to tie me up and slap me with food while my demon familiar watched and snickered.

"Don't look at me," Chupey said between pants. It was hot in here. "I would never support such blatant waste of good food."

True.

I turned my glower back toward Zane.

"Come on, Sloane," Zane said. "You need to at least try."

"This is the single most stupidest thing I've ever participated in," I said.

Zane sighed and lowered the tortilla shell. "Look. The Inferno doesn't often allow much, if any, downtime between trials. You're lucky to even have this morning as a break. You need to use this time to figure out a way to access that well of demonic magic lurking inside you. But you rely too much on your ability to kick ass."

"Damn straight."

Zane rolled his eyes. "That's the point of this exercise. I've removed your ability to punch and strangle me. If you can't resort to your fists, you might just reach for the unknown. It's worth a shot." He smacked me again.

My cheek stung. "Where did you even get this idea?"

"What? The tortilla?"

Smack.

I ground my teeth together. "Yeah. That."

"I got the idea from a trend on that clock app you humans love so much."

A trend? Clock app? What the fuck?

I thought about it for a few seconds, and when it clicked, I wanted to slap both him and myself.

He didn't really mean...?

Oh my god. He did.

I shook my head. "Since when did phones work in the Underworld?"

"They don't. Ryker isn't the only one to slip past the Styx and slum it topside, you know." He flashed a smug smile before slapping me across the face again. "Come on, Sloane. Use your power. Stop me."

I tried to access the same anger I'd used to form a portal, the same anger that had lashed out at Mobius, but each time I sensed the tingle of magic, the power would slip from my grasp.

My thoughts kept drifting to the impending trial. The first two trials had been polar opposites of one-another—a waterworld escape room and the floor is lava. What next? What could they possibly do to me next?

Smack.

"Goddammit!" I hissed. The tortilla didn't hurt so much as annoy me, but my cheek was beginning to sting.

"Maybe we should cut her," Chupey said.

"What the fuck, Chupey," I snapped. "You're supposed to be on my side."

Chupey shrugged. "I am on your side. Blood helps release magic."

"I don't think blood will help her. It's a mental game she's playing right now, and she's currently losing," Zane said.

"Did you just call me dumb?"

He raised the tortilla shell and slapped me across the face again. "What are you going to do about it, Sloane? Does it make you angry? Huh? Does it? Does it?"

Smack.

I growled and clenched my fists together. Cursing at Zane might make me feel better, but it wouldn't help me end torture by tortilla nor figure out a way to access my magic. Squeezing my eyes shut, I focused on the hum of power and reached for it.

Smack.

Zane's voice rose with his frustration. "Come on! You're a Dazamon! Unleash all that power onto me!"

"I'm a Daza-what-now?"

Chupey and Zane exchanged a look.

"A Dazamon. It's arguably one of the most powerful demon types in the Underworld," Chupey explained matter-of-factly. "That was what your father was, and that's what you are."

"But—" Zane interjected, "her human side must be hindering her demon. Making it too hard for her to tap into."

"That just means we have to work harder," Chupey answered.

Ah, shit. I didn't like the sound of that.

Nodding, Zane lifted the tortilla again. I never thought I'd get PTSD from food, but I was really starting to think Mexican food would be a big no-go for me after this.

I paused.

Who was I kidding?

Tacos would never make the no go list.

"Do I even want to know what you three stooges are up to?" Ryker's unexpected voice jolted me out of my head.

I cursed as the magic once again slipped from my grasp. I whirled around to find Ryker standing a few steps inside the doorway with his arms crossed over his chest. He wore a fitted shirt along with leather pants that showed off his muscular thighs. Somehow he made it work and the sight of him made my mouth water.

Which was ridiculous, because obviously I hated him.

Slightly behind him, Slade leaned on the door frame, with his hands shoved in his jeans' pockets and one leg crossed lazily over the other. Amusement dancing in his gaze. He'd paired his fitted jeans with a collared shirt and looked more like he should be walking the streets of Braton instead of sauntering into Hell's kitchen.

My hindsight didn't react to either of them. Interesting.

"Well?" Ryker raised a dark brow.

"Zane's helping me," I said. Really, none of this was his business. He didn't need to know a thing.

"By slapping you with carbs?" Confusion wrinkled his brow. "I know humans think carbs are the enemy, but this is kind of ridiculous, don't you think?"

Slade snorted.

"All it seems to be doing is irritating the fuck out of me," I admitted. "But I guess he can stop now, because you're here and you're way better at it."

Ryker straightened and unfolded his arms. With a few steps, he closed the distance between us. Instead of anger flashing in his gaze, he appeared amused. His lips turned up in the corners as he leaned down, impossibly close. "I'm better at a lot of things, princess."

God dammit, I hated when he called me that. And he knew I did. That was why he insisted on doing it more.

Despite my irritation, my stomach did that little flip thing it always did when he was around. And like always, I ignored it. "If you're so good, then help me unlock my magic."

When his grin grew, I knew immediately I made a mistake. Sliding his hands up my arms, his fingertips caressed my bare skin until they rested on my shoulders. I tugged on my bound hands, but the knots didn't budge.

Without a word, he slowly turned me back toward Zane.

"Ryker..." Zane said in warning with the limp tortilla drooping in his hand, but Ryker shushed him.

With his hands resting on my shoulders, and his body almost flush with mine, he asked, "Are you sure you want my help?"

I tried for a nonchalant shrug, not quite trusting my voice with the heat rolling off Ryker caressing my back. Memories of my dream spiraled up and more heat spread across my chest.

"Say it, Sloane," he growled in my ear. "Tell me you need me."

"I think I need a drink," Zane muttered.

Chupey whined.

I didn't want to hear what my demon familiar had to say about this, and Slade's silence near the doorway somewhere behind me felt very much like disapproval. "Okay, fine. Please help me."

Ryker's fingers dug into my shoulder a little, the only acknowledgement that he heard me. In the next breath, his magic poured over me. Hot and wet, like melted honey, his power coated my skin until it sunk in.

Ryker must've given Zane some silent signal, because my buddy started smacking me in the face again with that tortilla.

"Stop him, Sloane. Stop him with your magic." Ryker's order dissolved into his magic and surrounded me.

Smack.

This entire situation was ridiculous.

Smack.

Why on earth was I letting this jackass help me?

Smack.

His magic might feel good but he'd totally hold this over me later.

Smack.

I didn't want to owe him.

Smack.

I certainly didn't want his magic penetrating me.

Smack.

With a new drive of anger and Ryker's power to manipulate emotion amplifying my rage, I reached down and gripped my magic, throwing it out toward Zane.

"Ooo," the demon guard said with satisfaction. "That tickles."

I opened my eyes to find Zane's arm frozen mid-strike, tortilla in hand. He never landed the slap. The wide grin spread across his face told me I'd successfully accomplished using my magic. Now, could I do it again, without assistance, without being completely fired up with anger? That was the real question.

"Your father could freeze a legion of demons and slaughter them before they regained control," Ryker whispered near my ear, his breath fanning my hair and tickling my skin.

"I still don't get why you're helping me," I said.

"This will make everything more interesting." Ryker removed his hands and withdrew his magic.

The sudden loss of heat and power left me shivering. My magic had already slipped from my control, freeing Zane to move around, but when I reached for it again, it seemed more tangible, more readily available. Did this mean my power would come easier now? Would I still have control over my magic without his assistance?

Maybe next time, I could do more.

I turned to find Ryker already heading toward his friend and the exit. "You're going?"

"You should rest before the trial. Dazamon demon or not, there's no point in tapping yourself out before you've even started."

That comment made me wonder just how long he'd been standing there watching Zane and Chupey work on me and my magic.

"Rumor is the next trial is S'gor's, so you'll need all the help you can get," he went on as he headed for the door. He paused briefly at the doorway, then he turned to speak one last thing over his shoulder. "I'm a Bolvaath demon, by the way. If you even know what that means."

That you like to show up uninvited a lot?

Ryker walked out with Slade hurrying to catch him to his quickened pace. Their footsteps faded away in the distance.

When we were alone again, I turned to my two

hellish companions. "A Bolvaath? What the fuck is that?" I asked.

"A charmer, Sloane," Chupey explained in a harsh whisper. "A manipulator."

Well, didn't that just fit him to a tee.

"S'gor?" Zane's worried tone drew my focus back to him. "That's not good. I was hoping we'd have more time before her trial."

He and Chupey exchanged frowns, and my jitters began to bubble up again.

"Is that...*bad*?" My attempts to access my magic had momentarily taken my mind off of my impending trial and possible death, but now that the topic had come up, my nerves were about to hit an all time high record.

Staring at me, the seriousness on Zane's face only intensified. "It's definitely not good."

CHAPTER SIXTEEN

T he sand-colored magic of the third portal stared back at me, along with one of the council demons. S'gor, as Chupey identified her, was a sand demon known for hatred and war, but whatever waited for me on the other side couldn't be nearly as bad as the magma hellhole I'd survived yesterday. My arms and legs still burned and, despite nearly drinking enough water to drown me, I probably still lost about ten percent of my body weight from perspiration.

I ignored Ryker when I arrived at the portal this afternoon. I still ignored him, even though he only stood a few feet behind me waiting for me to step through the portal. The last thing I wanted to do was acknowledge how he helped me this morning or how he made me feel.

No, thank you.

As far as I was concerned, that little moment in the kitchen never happened.

"Anytime, princess," Ryker said, his voice somehow annoying and caressing at the same time.

Fucker. Without saying a thing, I stepped through the swirling magic and braced myself for the third trial.

I landed in a heap on hard-packed dirt, a dust cloud rising up around me. Pulling myself up and onto my feet, I straightened to find Ryker still a few feet away. He stood regally, not a spec of dirt on him. He must prance through the portals.

"What the hell?" I brushed the dirt off of my shirt and pants. "The trials are rigged."

"Don't blame the rest of us because you can't walk through portals, princess." His lips twitched.

I snarled at him and turned away to survey the area. We were in some sort of demonic style arena with no audience. A dry wind brushed over my skin and rustled up more loose dirt.

I looked down and frowned. I stood in the center of a marked circle. Glancing around confirmed the other remaining demons were in their own circles.

All except Mobius. He wasn't anywhere to be seen.

"Where's the large angry blue dude?"

"Mobius is no longer in the competition."

"What? Why?" This was the best news I'd received all day.

"Hard to compete with two broken hands."

I blanched. Would they disqualify me? Hardly seemed fair when I'd acted in self-defense. "I didn't do it."

"I know." Ryker's gaze darkened. "I did."

I opened my mouth and then closed it again. On the second try, I managed to get one word out. "Why?"

Ryker hesitated before he clamped his lips tightly together. Either he didn't want to say, or he didn't quite know the answer himself.

I glanced around and leaned over. "Won't that get you disqualified? He's not the type to remain silent."

"Mobius broke the rules of engagement first by attacking you. He was fair game."

Ah. Now that made sense. "You got rid of one of your biggest competitors at the first available opportunity."

Ryker glared at me.

"It's a smart move. I'm glad you did it." I toed the line that formed the circle around me. Sparks rose up from the dirt. "How'd you know Mobius attacked me, though? I didn't tell you his name."

"It wasn't hard to figure out. He's the only idiot who would say such a stupid line about a bitch dying in a hallway."

"Oh."

"And when I confronted him, he wouldn't shut up about it. About you. About what he planned to do to you when he got his hands on you again." Ryker glowered at the dirt in front of him as if it contained Mobius's face. "He should never have touched you."

Was that why Ryker had broken his hands specifically? I swallowed and turned my attention back to the marked circle. "Now if only I could figure this out."

"I wouldn't try stepping out prematurely," Ryker said.

"Out of the two of us, I'm fairly certain I'm not the one who struggles with doing anything *prematurely*," I snapped back.

Heat flashed in his gaze and a slow smile spread across his face. "Keep this attitude up, and I'm going to have to prove how wrong you are."

Was that a challenge? Did he not know me well at all? "Is that so? Don't over promise something you'll underdeliver."

"I will make you beg."

"I'll beg you to stop talking right now."

His smirk called me a liar without him having to open his mouth.

Whatever.

I waved at the circles. "How will we know when we can step out?"

He flashed his teeth at me, probably attempting to smile, and shrugged. "Probably when something heinously dangerous comes running out of the pit to attack us."

"What? Didn't we already prove our strength?"

"Strength? Strength has nothing to do with winning or losing a battle."

I narrowed my eyes.

"Strength isn't the only thing needed to win a battle," Ryker amended.

I turned away from him to study the arena again. High walls enclosed the dry space as empty stands looked on. I'd never been to Rome, never set eyes on the colosseum in person, but if I had to bet, based on images and movies, I'd say this arena was what the colosseum would've looked like before time turned it into ruins. Only this arena was much, much larger.

"So, they're testing us on tactics," I said. Lovely. Because I had years of training in battle tactics.

Ugh.

He nodded. "You know what a good tactic is for winning a battle?"

"It's not cutting down the competition," I said. That would be a wasted effort.

"No, though we might have to worry about that with the others." He paused and looked over at the remaining competitors. "Even with Mobius out of the picture."

I quickly counted them.

Only twelve remained in the competition, in addition to Ryker and me.

"You want to team up?" I guessed.

"Why yes, Sloane. Thank you. I thought you'd never ask." His dry tone would've dehydrated raisins.

"I'm surprised you don't want to team up with your demonic buddies over there."

"Them?" He grunted. "They're more likely to stab me in the back when the first opportunity arises."

I looked over at the others again. None of them stood out the way Mobius had, but I couldn't let that fool me. These demons had survived the previous trials. I couldn't afford to dismiss them for the very real danger they represented.

The air in front of Ryker shifted and sparked, and suddenly, a long sword materialized in his palm. He gripped the hilt, grinning with approval, while I stared dumbstruck at what I'd just witnessed. It was like some deadly magic trick.

"Now this is what I'm talking about!" Ryker laughed, swiping the blade through the air.

Energy buzzed up and down my arms, and the magic pushed through the space in front of me, too. Instinctually, I held out my hands, and to my shock, two daggers emerged out of the nothing, just as Ryker's sword had.

"Looks like Christmas came early," he said.

My fingers tightened around the leather handles, still unsure how this was possible. "Weapons can't be brought into the trials but..."

"No one ever said anything about weapons being sent in."

"Hmm..."

"Would you rather fight these bastards empty handed?"

"No."

"You're smarter than I thought then."

"You're not worried that I'll stab you in the back either?" I asked Ryker, making slashing motions with my new toys. The more I played with them, the more I liked how light and easy to wield they were.

"You won't."

"How are you so sure?" I don't know why I bothered to ask. He'd already answered a similar question earlier during the magma trials—my mortal character flaw.

He smirked as if he followed my entire internal conversation. "As I mentioned before, you're half human and one hundred percent too sentimental."

And again, he made my compassion sound like a weakness. I rolled my eyes.

I didn't have a chance to clap back. A loud roar rocked the arena and shook the ground. Dust rose up. Heavy footsteps thundered down and grew more intense with each step.

Something wicked this way comes.

Ryker pursed his lips and gripped the hilt of his sword. The humor that had tugged at his lips disappeared. The wind played with his dark hair and the sheer strength and beauty of the demon standing nearby struck me.

Not the time, Sloane.

The monster stepped into the arena through a large cloud of dust. Standing around twenty feet tall, a monstrous boar-like giant loomed over us. With hooved feet, he stood on two muscular legs and wore a tattered loincloth to hide his monster junk. Tough hide and coarse fur covered his bare chest.

My gaze kept traveling upward, more horrified by the second.

His face.

My brain short-circuited.

He had a snout like a boar, a singular large eye like a cyclops, and instead of hair, he had long, snake-like tentacles.

"What the fuck is that?" I asked.

"Borca."

"Who? What?"

"He's the Fomorian giant no one likes to talk about."

Borca dropped his giant head back and roared. The tentacles around his face spread out and shrieked, creating an eerie harmony that raised every single hair on my body. His giant torso contracted showing lines of corded pectoral muscles and abs that looked like they tried to punch free of his body.

"Uh...How do we kill it?"

"Quickly." Ryker toed the line that drew up the circle around him. Light shimmered and magic snapped out. Ryker jerked back with a hiss.

I bit my lip and held back the snarky comment

threatening to bubble out of my mouth. Now was definitely not the time to verbally spar with Ryker.

Instead, I focused on Borca. The trials so far had been pretty rigged, favoring demons who grew up in the Underworld. I couldn't even get upset about that, because it made sense. The ruler should know the customs, language, and history of the people or things they ruled.

If only Ryker hadn't run off to rat me out to the council. I would've had two weeks to cram this information into my stubborn brain.

Oh well.

Lamenting wouldn't help me win this battle.

How could I possibly beat the giant in front of me? I'd barely escaped Mobius who was less than half the size.

Borca had one eye like the cyclops from Greek mythology. Would stabbing him through the eye, like how Odysseus and his men killed the cyclops, be the key to defeating the giant?

Borca also had a massive dong, and that little tattered loincloth did little to hide the swinging. Nothing was left to my imagination, especially not at this angle. The giant's giant penis was ridiculous, but the groin was also typically a vulnerable location. Would that be the key to defeating him?

There was also a tale about David and Goliath. I couldn't quite remember that one, but there was a slingshot involved, wasn't there? And a rock?

"Do you have a plan in mind?" I yelled over to Ryker.

"Don't die."

"No, seriously."

"I am being serious. The first phase should be avoiding death and letting the rest risk their lives while we await an opening."

"Are we going for the eye?"

"The eye, the throat." Ryker's expression remained grim. "Hell, I'd even suggest his junk if I didn't think it would just piss him off more."

A giant portal opened and spat out a number of small figures.

A small demon who looked part Xoloitzcuintle, part mutt, and part three-year-old toddler with attachment issues, froze in the shadow of Borca.

Chupey turned to me, eyes wide with fear, and my heart constricted.

No!

The circle of magic that contained me snapped out of existence and I ran.

"Sloane," Ryker barked.

I gripped my daggers and sprinted, my focus only on my dog—my *friend*. Panic punched my lungs. I had to get to Chupey. He was all I had.

Borca turned his gargantuan body around as the small demons scattered.

They must be everyone else's familiars.

I screamed. Chupey whipped his head around, his snout lifting up and up as he took in Borca.

Chupey bolted, running for his life.

Almost in slow motion, yet covering so much distance, Borca knelt down and reached forward.

Everything unfolded as if I was watching it on television, out of my own body, my terror making it hard to grasp onto reality.

This couldn't be happening.

I was still too far away.

As Chupey's terrified eyes met mine, my pulse thundered against my eardrums.

I had to get to him *right now*.

Borca swooped up my familiar and shoveled him into his open mouth, the big bulb of his Adam's apple bobbing in his throat as he swallowed.

A bone-shattering scream ripped from my lips. I screeched at Borca and something broke inside me. Something hidden deep within snapped and a long-slumbering power unfurled. Magic rose up, hot, sticky, and powerful.

Chupey was all I had. All I loved in this world, and right now he was inside the giant.

Power ripped from inside my body and clamped onto the monster in front of me.

Borca froze as if suspended in time.

I had no idea what I was doing or how I was doing it, but the power was coming from an untapped well inside of me, one that I'd never accessed until now. I'd stunned Mobius yesterday, and tickled Zane with my magic this morning, but this was different, this was next level, and I had no idea how to wield it.

Dazamon.

This was the power of a Dazamon. And it ripped uncontrollably from me, clamping Borca in place as I closed the distance between us.

Since Borca was still kneeling, his face was close enough to reach. I planted my foot on his outstretched hand and launched myself toward his face. I slashed and stabbed and hacked at his throat, over and over again, as blood sprayed out and soaked my clothes.

I cut a seam into the side of Borca's neck until I could reach in and pull Chupey out.

When my fingertips brushed against a familiar shape, I seized it and pulled with all my strength. In an instant, my familiar's limp body fell to the dusty ground covered in blood and saliva.

Please don't be dead.

To my relief, Chupey stirred, and a low whine escaped his snout. I slid down the giant's neck and landed a few feet away, near my demon dog. As I scooped him into my arms, he felt so much smaller to me then, fragile, and my heart ached.

I'd almost lost him.

Chupey shook and hacked against my chest, drawing in deep shaking breaths, and in that moment, my invisible hold on the monster shattered.

Borca bellowed, rearing back and spraying blood

from his massacred neck. Somehow, I hadn't hit anything vital because he didn't fall down and die.

And he wanted revenge.

He threw out his meaty fist. I tucked Chupey closer, curled myself around him, and rolled out of the way just as Borca's fist pounded the dirt, right where we'd just been.

As Borca swiped the ground with his hand toward us, kicking up dust, I pushed Chupey to safety.

That left me in the monster's path.

"Go!" I barely got out the word before I was slammed by Borca's attack, The air punched out of my lungs as I was tossed sideways.

"Sloane!"

I could've sworn I heard Ryker's frantic cry, but pain wracked my body and I hit the ground hard. Maybe I'd imagined Ryker's voice. All I knew for sure was that every time I breathed in, it felt like I inhaled broken glass and my head whirled from the lack of oxygen flowing to it. But when a massive dark shadow traveled over me, I knew I had only seconds to move again, or risk becoming flattened like a pancake.

Pushing to my knees, I spotted Borca's fist barreling down on me again, so I twisted out of the way, crouched, and launched my battered body at his hand. I slammed into his fist. Before I slid off, I stabbed my daggers into his hand, using them like little pick axes to stay in place.

I sure as fuck wasn't graceful.

Hanging onto my daggers for dear life, I scrambled to adjust my grip on my weapons and get my bearings. By some miracle, I hoisted my tired body up his wrist as he lifted his arm again. He roared and the booming sound bounced off the area all around me.

Embracing the entirety of my demonic magic, wearing it like a shield and energy booster, I climbed up the creature again, using my daggers to help me while hurting him in the process. His blood coated every inch of me, making my grip slippery and harder to manage.

Still bellowing, Borca tried to grab me with his uninjured hand. Fear gripped me as I looked down at the ground too far away to jump and live. I had nowhere to go.

But I didn't have time to think about it because as his fingers reached for me, my hold on one of my daggers slipped, and I was forced to launch myself at his chest.

I smacked into him hard, enough to temporarily darken my vision. I blindly stabbed out with my other knife, embedding the blade in his abdomen. With no time to catch my breath, the blade began to slice downward, taking me with it.

The ground was rushing toward me too fast.

Fuuucccckkk!

More blood rained down on me, and I squeezed my eyes shut, knowing I was about to break every bone in my body—if I somehow survived this.

At the last second, I opened them again to see a blur of movement racing toward me.

Then, instead of death, something slammed into me, and suddenly I was tumbling across the dirt again —this time with a stranger on top of me.

My blurry vision adjusted just enough to see Ryker's handsome face staring down at me, full of worry, but as I opened my mouth to tell him to get off, I saw the Broca swaying, about to topple over.

Right on top of us.

Ryker must have seen the terror in my eyes because his gaze whipped over his shoulder. Without hesitation, he wrenched me against him and rolled us. Borca's body crashed to the ground, too close for comfort. Aftershocks rippled across the dirt and raised a mushroom cloud of dust.

I coughed and waved at the dirt in the air.

"Are you out of your fucking mind?" Ryker gasped, chest heaving as he climbed off me.

He'd saved me. My biggest competition. My sworn enemy. My most hated adversary.

"I'm starting to think I am," I wheezed. Everything hurt. *Everything*. And the amount of dirt in the air wasn't helping me catch my breath.

Ryker didn't offer a hand. Instead, he squinted at the giant's unmoving body. "So much for sticking to the plan."

I scramble to my feet. "Is he dead?"

"Very." He glanced over at me and smirked. "Not too bad, princess."

Some of the other competitors swarmed around Borca's head, stabbing deeply. Others still cowered around the edges of the arena, clutching their familiars to their chests.

My heart pounded from both the adrenaline of the fight and from Ryker's intervention and what it could mean. I didn't understand why he'd saved me when letting me die would give him a clear line to the throne he wanted.

I continued to stare at him, my body buzzing, my mind spinning in two opposite directions.

He was competition. I was supposed to despise him.

But...

He eyed me suspiciously. "What?"

I closed the distance between us, gripped a handful of his shirt, and hauled him close. My mouth crashed onto his, my need to taste him overcoming every other thought. I half expected him to rip himself away from me, but instead, he kissed me back with just as much intensity. Groaning, his tongue wrestled with mine, demanding dominance.

And though part of my brain screamed at me, the rest had me plastering my body to his. His fingers raked through my hair and tugged hard enough to have me gasping, but the pain only ignited the desire already swirling inside me.

This felt good. *He* felt good.

I didn't know how or when I'd become so drawn to Ryker, but damn... I couldn't seem to stay away from him or keep my hands to myself when he was near.

I clung to him, closing my arms around his strong torso and hiking my leg over his hip. Apparently, I wanted to climb him.

And that wasn't all I wanted.

I wanted to taste him, tease him, and claim him. Heat danced along my skin with need. My scar burned. My core ached. If I didn't have him right now, I might die.

Ryker yanked his head back.

I looked into his emerald-green eyes and my breath caught. His gaze held the same need and hunger thrumming in my veins.

He drew in a ragged breath and ran his calloused thumb along my cheek. "You're not allowed to die."

"Is that your way of saying I can have the throne?" I panted.

"The throne will be mine. Just like you will be. Just like you are." He leaned forward and snagged my mouth for another intense kiss.

"I'm...yours?" I raised an eyebrow.

"You're mine." He visibly shook himself. "Mine to kill."

Son of a bitch!

"Then get off." I shoved him away. "You can't

distract me with your good looks and that thing you do with your tongue."

He raised his eyebrows and stepped back. "That thing I do with my tongue?"

Heat flushed my cheeks, but I refused to look away. My body still ached with an unanswered need. He was such an ass, yet I wanted him. God, I wanted him so badly it hurt.

A sleek figure raced over and skidded to a stop at Ryker's feet. A smaller, leaner version of Chupey looked up at Ryker, adoration clear on its face. I recognized his familiar immediately—Zi.

"This is Zi'rel," he introduced us, and the demon dog responded by turning to me and snarling. She flashed long, blood-stained teeth.

I stepped back. "What's your problem?"

"You should step aside," she purred, her voice low and smooth and in complete contrast to Chupey's. "You are weak and useless compared to my master."

Everybody's a critic.

The lingering heat in my veins aching for Ryker faded away, replaced with ice. Step aside? Me? Not fucking likely. "Pretty sure I'm the one that just hacked into Borca's throat. I wouldn't be so quick to insult me."

My own familiar emerged from the dust cloud and slinked over to me. He said nothing, pressing his blood and saliva soaked body into my leg. He must really be rattled to stay quiet. Or maybe watching me try to hump Ryker through our clothes horrified him so much he lost his ability to speak.

A portal snapped open a few feet away.

"And, just so we're clear. Stepping aside? That's not happening," I told Zi'rel before turning to Ryker. I jabbed my finger into his hard chest. "And the only thing that's yours is the failure you'll feel when I win my rightful place on the throne."

Not waiting for a response, I spun on my heel and stalked through the portal, Chupey close behind me.

CHAPTER SEVENTEEN

Chupey shivered in the standing shower as I ran the soapy, warm water over him. Saliva, blood, and little chunks of Borca's flesh pooled at his feet. He hadn't said anything as we emerged from the portal and stalked off toward my room. He didn't even beg for food.

"You're going to be okay," I said, running my hand down the tuft of fur on his head.

He shook, tiny vibrations, and his tail remained curled up under his belly. Poor guy. He'd seen the inside of Borca's mouth and throat, and had to have thought that was how things would end.

Rage simmered just below my skin at the thought. I couldn't let it out. I couldn't unleash the fury boiling within me. My anger wouldn't solve anything right now. If anything, it would only scare Chupey more.

My demon familiar whined and bent his legs, crouching lower in the shower.

"Can you sense my anger?"

He jerked his head up and down.

"Sorry, bud." I ran more warm water over him and rubbed the blood free from his coat. "I'm trying to calm down."

He turned and tucked his snout under my arm, sliding his head up until his cold, wet nose reached my armpit. It tickled. But Chupey wasn't looking for laughter, he wanted comfort.

I turned the showerhead off and grabbed an extra-large towel. Wrapping the fluffy fabric around my demon familiar, I hauled him out of the shower and cradled him in my lap. I wrapped my arms around him and held him. Just held him. Though the trial had ended as soon as we left through the portal, part of me still needed reassurance that Chupey was safe. Alive.

"You're everything to me, Chupey," I mumbled into his wet fur. "You've always been there for me. Ever since I was an angsty teenager trying to survive high school, you've been my emotional support. You were there for me when Suzy Jenkins made me doubt my worth and question whether my ass really was too fat. You were there for me when I lost my v-card to that prick who-shall-not-be-named. You were the first one I told when I got accepted into my first pick university, and you were the one I cried on when I realized I couldn't afford to go. You were there for me when

Mom passed away. You've always been in my corner."
Tears spilled from my eyes, but I kept holding Chupey.
"You're my emotional support demon and I'd be lost
without you." I licked my lips.

"When I saw you disappear into Borca's mouth," I
continued. "When he started to swallow...Something
broke inside of me. I've lost so much, I couldn't lose
you. Do you understand Chupey? My mortality might
make me weaker than some of these douche-canoes,
but you are my true weakness."

He'd stopped shaking and rested his head on my
shoulders.

"I love you," I whispered into his fur. "And if you
ever let some demon turds kidnap you to throw you
into a demonic trial again, I will absolutely lose my
shit."

Chupey hacked, his dog equivalent of a laugh. "I
love you, too, Sloane."

I pulled back and ruffled his mohawk. "So, I'm not
just some job to complete for my deceased dad?"

"Woman, you stopped being just a job the moment
you fed me some of your bacon."

I laughed. I couldn't help it. Giggles erupted from
my lips, and I ended up cackling like some maniacal
witch.

"It wasn't that funny," Chupey said.

"It's the stress." I wiped the tears from my eyes.
"How are you feeling?"

Chupey wiggled free of the towel and stepped

back. His limbs no longer shook and his mohawk poofed out like he'd had a professional blow-out. "I'm better."

"Good enough to go get some food?"

Chupey snorted.

Guess that was a yes.

After I showered and changed into clean clothes, we headed for the dining hall. I unceremoniously dropped the outfit I wore to the last trial in the garbage. There were some things not worth salvaging. That included blood-soaked gear with Borca bits smushed into the fabric.

The anger still simmered below the surface, ready to erupt, but having a hug from Chupey grounded me a little. Yes, he'd almost died. Yes, I'd absolutely lost my mind with rage and unleashed some unknown Dazamon magic inside me. But Chupey survived and the magic wasn't a bad thing.

If only I could call it at will. I needed to work on my demon power crap before the next trial.

But first, food.

The grand entrance to the dining hall loomed ahead, illuminated by firelight from the torches.

Ryker stepped out of nowhere and blocked my path.

I skidded to a halt and Chupey growled.

"If you know what's best for you," I started. "You won't get in the way of my familiar and food."

Ryker smirked and stepped to the side. "Go ahead, Chupe. We won't be long."

Chupey hesitated, glancing between me and the food.

"It's okay, Chupe," Ryker said. "On my life, I wish her no harm...right now."

I rolled my eyes.

Chupey remained frozen and visibly torn.

"Go, Chupey. I'll be fine," I said. Poor thing just needed some bacon.

With a pained last look, Chupey trotted ahead and disappeared into the dining hall.

"On a scale of one to ten, how angry are you?" Ryker asked.

"I'm at a motherfucking eleven."

Ryker nodded.

"And you? How do you feel about them using our familiars as bait?"

"I'm livid."

"Really?" I raised an eyebrow. "Because from where I'm standing, you look pretty relaxed."

Ryker turned to me then, fully, and met my gaze. The green in his eyes flashed and flickered like they held the fires of Hell, and in the next blink he had me pinned to the wall.

"I'm livid," he repeated. "Once I'm Lucifer, S'gor will pay for this."

I lifted my chin. "Once I'm Lucifer, you mean."

He narrowed his eyes and his gaze dropped to my lips. He leaned down, impossibly close, and my memories of his mouth on mine rose up and made warmth spread through my body.

I licked my lips.

Ryker stared at my mouth, transfixed by the movement. I couldn't let him kiss me. If he laid those plump lips on me, I'd dry hump him in this very hallway. Too much stress, too much built-up tension...I'd erupt and then I'd have to deal with his smug face until I finally beat him.

I cleared my throat and looked away. "Is there something you wanted?"

"There's a whole lot of things I want right now." He leaned in, pressing his hips forward so his erection dug into me.

"Jesus..."

"I'm not Jesus." Ryker chuckled and shook his head. "I'm not God, either. But you say the word, Sloane, you bob that pretty little head of yours, and I can be your god tonight."

Part of me wanted to whimper and melt into his warmth. Heat already pooled low in my belly. It would be so easy to say yes. So easy to fall in bed with him and get lost in pleasure.

And not so easy in the morning. He'd be such a pain in the ass the next day.

"You were hanging out, waiting to intercept me in

the hallway like some two-bit villain from a B-list movie. Why?"

"A two-bit villain?" He raised an eyebrow.

"Now you're just stalling, or evading."

Ryker pulled back, taking his glorious heat and massive erection with him. "The next trial is tomorrow," he said.

"Okay..."

"They normally have a break between the third and fourth, an intermission of sorts, but they'd decided to plow ahead. I wanted you to know."

"Why? I'm your competition. Wouldn't it be best to hide the information from me, so I miss the trial and you win by default?" And wouldn't Chupey get this information anyway? Ryker didn't need to personally relay the schedule change to me. It was almost as if he used it as an excuse to see me.

I narrowed my eyes. What was he up to?

Ryker tsked and shook his head. "I don't want you to miss the trial, Sloane. I don't want to win by default."

"Why not?"

He leaned in. "I look forward to the competition."

"You really do have issues."

"Just say the word, Sloane, and I'll show you some of them." He winked and walked away, leaving me stuttering in the hallway, torn between running after him like some needy bitch and finding Chupey and food.

This time, my familiar and food won the internal debate. What scared me was how close I came to running after the demon. How close I came to saying yes.

CHAPTER EIGHTEEN

I ran through the gate to the portal cliff and skidded to a halt. Chupey bumped into the back of my legs, and I took a few steps forward to avoid falling over like a dead tree. The sight of the same six portals greeted me, along with the Council of Six, Ryker, and his familiar. Other than that, the entire cliff was empty. The other competitors, their familiars, and the cheering squads were gone.

Ryker and Zi'rel turned at our entrance.

"Where's everyone else?" I asked.

"They dropped out," Ryker said. He wore dark, ripped jeans, with chains and a black T-shirt that emphasized his strong chest and wide shoulders.

Zi'rel sniffed in my direction before turning her nose up in the air.

"What? Why?" I started walking again, heading toward the fourth portal, Chupey trotting along beside me. The inside of this one swirled with a mixture of purple and pink.

"Are you upset to have less competition?" He raised a dark eyebrow.

"Of course not." Though I certainly wished he'd dropped out, too. "But why?"

Ryker shrugged. "Who fucking knows. After seeing us with the Borca, they must've realized they didn't stand a chance."

"After seeing *us*?" I laughed. "That's funny because I distinctly remember being the one to slice that monster up like it was a Thanksgiving turkey. You were nowhere to be found until the end."

Now it was his turn to laugh.

Having the others quit brought good news and bad. Less competition, but now it really was just down to me and Ryker. And only one of us could win. "Maybe you should do the smart thing and drop out too. Save yourself the embarrassment."

He smirked and shook his head.

"Mark my words, Ryker. The throne will be mine."

We stopped a few feet from the portal. The Council of Six remained on their dais, motionless except for turning their heads to track our progress. I learned their names, but Zane was still filling me in on their backstories. I already knew Malachi, Ifrit, and S'gor from the first three trials. And S'gor had a lot to answer for. I wouldn't forgive what that demon did to Chupey anytime soon. The other three council demons were Ba'al, Gwyn, and Moloch, but I wasn't sure who was who. Zane had provided descriptions, of course, but with all the info-dumping, I couldn't recall which bio belonged to which demon.

One of the demons, with glistening white hair cascading down his back, stepped from the line to stand beside the swirling fourth portal. His white horns sparkled under the glaring sun. He didn't wear a shirt, choosing not to hide his bulging chest muscles, chiseled abs, and smooth, tanned skin. A furry loincloth with a studded leather belt hid the family giblets but left very little to the imagination. There was nothing little about him.

"Do you want a bib?" Ryker leaned in to ask.

"What?"

"You're drooling."

"I am not."

"You kind of are," Chupey added.

I glared down at my familiar. "Not helpful, Chupey."

The council demon waited patiently while we discussed my drooling, his smirk growing.

I threw my hands up.

"My name is Ba'al," the demon said, his voice a deep purr. "If you're successful in your claim to the throne, I very much look forward to working with you."

His smile was sinful. I swallowed a groan and stepped through the portal.

Ryker followed, but our familiars didn't.

"Let me guess, that guy's an incubus or some sort of sex demon?" What I really wanted to ask was why male demons seemed obsessed with wearing loincloths, but I wasn't really ready for the answer, so I kept my mouth shut.

Ryker's grin nearly split his face. "You did remarkably well at repelling his magic. I rocked a hard-on for three days when I first met him."

I widened my eyes.

"And I don't even swing that way."

Squeezing my eyes shut, I tried really hard not to think of Ryker swinging anything.

And failed.

I shook my head and turned to survey the fourth trial. "So, this must be some sort of sex trial. You're so going to lose."

Ryker chuffed out a laugh and stepped forward to stand beside me on an uneven tiled path leading through a field of thick, lush grass and wildflowers. A thick pink haze floated through the air like smoke, carrying with it subtle floral scents.

"I guess we follow the path?" I asked.

"Did you want to hold hands?"

"Fuck off."

He smirked and walked along beside me, his shoulder brushing mine.

"This path isn't wide enough for both of us." I leaned into him, giving a little push.

He didn't budge. "And yet, I don't feel comfortable

with you walking behind me and I doubt you'd prefer the reverse." He shrugged and kept walking beside me. "So here we are."

We crested the hill. The path led into a valley, surrounded by trees. A brook babbled in the distance and the pink haze grew thicker as we descended into the valley.

"Did you mean everything you said when we first met?" I asked. "About my family?"

"I've said a lot about your family. You'll have to be more specific."

"About hating all of us. About blaming us all for the actions of one man. One demon."

"You're still benefiting from his actions, Sloane," he said. "And my family is still paying for them."

I looked away. Somehow, over the last few trials, Ryker and I had become...something else. Not friends, exactly, but no longer enemies, either. Not quite. "For what it's worth, I would step aside and let you have the throne if I didn't need it."

His step faltered, but he quickly recovered before he whispered, "To save your life."

"Yeah." My gut twisted. I really did feel for Ryker, despite hating his guts, of course.

"And I can't step aside for you, either," he said, after a lengthy pause. "I can't let go of my life's vendetta, no matter how much you like that thing I do with my tongue."

I snorted, but my humor quickly dissolved when a thought struck me. "Did you kill my father?"

"What?" He looked at me, expression incredulous. "No. Never. Even if I wanted to gain the throne that way, my power would have never matched your father's. A fully realized Dazamon demon is near untouchable." He shook his head. "Your father's talent lay in battle, something I suspect you inherited. My plan had always been this. I've waited a long time for the Inferno."

"No one has really told me much about his death. Chupey didn't have any answers." If he was so badass, how did someone manage to kill him? Something didn't add up, but no one was talking.

"That's because there's not much to know," Ryker said.

I frowned. "What do you mean? You said it was grisly. Surely that means there's something to discuss. Something to know or learn from the evidence left."

"Discuss? Yes. Gain helpful information? No. His room was bathed in his blood and there were severed body parts. We never recovered the rest of his body, nor did we get any evidence or clues to who was responsible."

I opened my mouth to ask more when soft laughter trickled up the path and interrupted my thoughts. Warmth spread through my chest, my heart thumped heavy, and my breathing quickened in response. Thoughts of my father and his death slipped away.

Ryker cursed.

I frowned and turned to him. A pink glow had replaced the normal blaze of his green eyes. "What's the problem?"

For the first time since the trials began, I felt good. Real good.

Speaking of real good, Ryker looked particularly delicious right now, despite the whole "I hate your family and spent my life preparing to take the throne" speech.

As if sensing my turmoil, Ryker reached out and quickly snagged my hand in his. He had large, warm hands, rough from calluses and hard work. His skin tingled along mine, his seductive magic sinking in.

I jerked my hand out of his. "Stop it."

"It's not me." He scowled and grabbed my hand again. "It's pixie dust, Sloane."

"Bullshit. You can control me with touch. I knew you'd stoop to demonic shenanigans to win." I stared down at our joined hands. Despite my words, my hand in his felt...nice.

Asshole.

He probably made me feel that way.

"I'm not controlling you, Sloane. I don't want to win that way."

I narrowed my eyes. Could I trust him? So far, he'd never lied to me. He might be a total jerk, but he was an honest jerk.

"I promise," he said.

Fine. He didn't seem too pleased to hold my hand either, so obviously something more was going on here. I just wished I wasn't working with limited information all the time. "So, what is it?"

"Pixie dust. They'll try to seduce us."

"Who?" No one else was in sight.

"Anyone and everyone we come upon. This is Ba'al's territory. I knew the second he stepped forward this would be a test on seduction and charm."

I snorted. Ryker certainly lacked the latter of those two things.

"This is serious, Sloane. If you fall for their charm, their seduction, you'll end up lost here, getting fucked to death. I wouldn't wish that fate on my worst enemy."

Yeah, that sounded fantastic and terrible at the same time.

"You'll forget to eat, drink, sleep. You'll become a shell of yourself," he said.

I pursed my lips. "How do we get through it?"

"A good leader won't fall prey to lower demon shenanigans. We have to be stronger than their magic."

Easier said than done.

Ryker's expression softened. "You're so lucky I need you."

That surprised me.

"The easiest way to defy pixy dust is to anchor yourself to someone else. For me, that's you. Looks like we're getting through this one together."

"Again."

He dipped his chin.

"Because I'm yours?"

His hand tightened on mine, but he didn't say anything.

We walked in silence, hand in hand as the scene in front of us unfolded through the thick pink haze. Silken pillows, soft furs, and plush rugs lined the bank of a slow babbling river. Naked bodies lay across the fabrics, entwined and writhing. Soft moans and humming filled the air along with the slap of bodies coming together.

A man bent a woman over, plunging into her from behind while spanking her round ass. She groaned in pleasure as each thrust rocked her.

"Fuck." Ryker paled and his grip on my hand tightened more.

I didn't blame him. We were walking through a real-life orgy.

Hands reached out and caressed our legs. A woman grabbed my free hand and winked, trying to pull me onto the large cushion and onto her curvy body.

The pink haze encircled me, enticing, seductive. It had been so long since I let myself relax, since I felt the warm embrace of a lover and let them take me over the edge.

Everything had been chaotic leading up to now —the fights, the diagnosis, the unknown. Every time I felt like I finally got my feet on solid ground, everything shifted. I'd pivoted the soles right off my shoes.

Maybe if I just laid down on the pillows and let these sex fiends have their way with me, I could finally find a sense of calm in this chaotic world.

Ryker tightened his grip on my hand. "We need to get over the river."

Right now, I needed to get him inside me.

I stumbled.

What a terrible thought. I hated Ryker. He'd tried to use me as a coffee table and made me clean his shoes. He challenged me for *my* throne, the one thing that could save my life. I despised him.

Didn't I?

Glancing sideways, I studied the man walking beside me.

"Don't look at me like that," he growled.

"Like what?"

"Like you haven't eaten for days and just stumbled upon an all-you-can-eat buffet."

Heat wound through my body. "I am hungry."

His lips twitched. "Stop it."

"What's the matter, Ryker? Afraid you might like it?"

"Oh, I'd enjoy every second of fucking you and making you beg for more." He flashed his teeth at me. "But we need to get out of here first."

I swiped at my brow and batted a man's hand away from my crotch. "You think you're strong enough to resist all of this?" I waved my hand at my body and rocked my hips in the air.

I meant it as a joke, but the fire in Ryker's gaze froze me on the spot.

"The second we get out of here, Sloane," he warned. "The second we walk through that gate..." He jabbed his finger in the air to aggressively point at the path ahead.

My feet hit the cold water and splashed up my legs, but the river did little to extinguish the fire raging inside me.

"Tell me," I said. "Tell me what you want to do to me."

Ryker pulled me into the hard planes of his body, his gaze dancing like the lick of firelight, his erection pressing into my hip. "Why should I tell you that?"

"Huh?" I swallowed. Blinking didn't clear the fog in my head.

"Why should I tell you, when I can show you?" Without warning, he pulled me forward and carried me through the waiting pink swirl of a portal.

CHAPTER NINETEEN

I want him written on my skin.

And the feeling didn't stop when we made it through the portal. On the other side, the world was exactly as I'd left it, except I had changed. That sliver of calm I'd fought to find in Ba'al's territory clicked into place when I felt Ryker's hand on my wrist, squeezing.

A tug brought me further into the cage of his arms. I tilted my head up automatically and he pressed his lips to mine. That tongue swirled in devious circles along the seam of my mouth, and I opened for him easily. Quickly.

He dragged me closer to his powerful body and kissed the air from my lungs. I felt him, hard and pressing against me.

"I'm going to show you, Sloane," he warned. "Show you all the things I've wanted to do to you."

"Good," I said against his mouth.

My groan echoed back to me as he pressed me into the wall. Grinding into me, he deepened the kiss and made me forget everything for a few minutes. Or an hour. We staggered along a hallway. I didn't realize the portal had spat us out inside the castle until he had us at the door to my room. Ryker kicked out, pushing his way into the room with such force I was surprised something didn't break.

Chupey whined and slunk out the door before we closed it. Apparently, he knew when to choose his battles, and trying to talk us out of this most definitely would be a battle. We'd been heading down this path this whole time.

The heat radiating off Ryker rivaled the scorching burn from the air in the second trial, and I wouldn't have had it any other way.

"Are you sure?" he asked.

"Absolutely." If he stopped now, I might die.

"Thank fuck." Ryker pushed me down onto the bed, his tongue between my lips and my heart threatening to burst out of my chest. My veins were alight at the thought of what he planned to do, and what I wanted him to do to me.

"You're going to scream for me," he said, nudging my knees apart to settle between them. He slid a hand between us to touch me, and I arched into him. "You're going to beg, and scream."

Damn it if I wanted him to make good on those boasts.

"Do you want me to be a good girl, or a bad girl?" I asked breathlessly as he bent to nip his way down my neck.

"I want you to be whatever the fuck you want."

I liked his answer.

I especially liked when he tugged my shorts down and slid his fingers across the edge of my panties. I was already wet and ready for him.

But I *loved* the way he growled as he teased me. My blood had turned to liquid honey, my limbs tingling with anticipation, my body humming with need. My panties hit the floor along with my shorts, and Ryker pressed his fingers to my naked core. He started slow, painstakingly slow, building up speed and pressure.

"*Oh, God.*"

Ryker chuckled darkly in the back of his throat. "Sorry, princess, but he's got no place here."

As if to prove his point, Ryker twisted his fingers inside me so slowly I whimpered, shaking beneath him.

I was a few pumps away from combusting and he hadn't even taken his clothes off yet.

"This has got to go." I tugged at his pants, my voice commanding and leaving no room for argument. Instead of complying, he caught my hand and shifted it down to cup the large ridge of his erection. He was so hard right now.

"How do I know this isn't some kind of trick of yours?" Ryker pushed up on his elbows to watch me, his face greedy and his tongue flicking out to wet his lips. "To get me to lower my guard so you can gut me?"

"Don't even joke," I said breathlessly. And he was joking. He had my number and knew betrayal wasn't in my playbook.

To emphasize my point, I squeezed his package and shifted to grab his lower lip between my teeth. Without missing a beat, Ryker groaned and drove his fingers into me faster, making my head spin. The echoes of the seduction trial faded away, leaving only me and Ryker and the heat of our kisses.

"You are such an asshole," I panted out.

He grinned, leaning down close to me to say, "That's what you like about me."

My entire body arched as he continued to build the need inside of me. I needed him, now. Riding his hand wasn't going to be enough.

Ryker kept up the motion as he quickly shed his pants and boxers, freeing his erection, and with his piercing green gaze, he watched me as he brought his free hand to his huge length and stroked.

The man was gifted in more ways than one.

"Are you going to keep me waiting all day, showing off?" I asked. "Or are you going to do something?"

"What do you want me to do?" he asked.

Everything. "You promised to show me."

"Exactly."

He continued to circle his thumb on me and soon I lost complete control. The noises leaving my throat weren't entirely human, especially when he moved his other hand to squeeze my breasts and pinch my nipples. The moment I came, exploding through a tidal wave of pleasure that went on for much longer than normal, I opened my eyes to find Ryker lined up with my core.

"Sloane..." he groaned.

He pressed inside of me slowly, torturously, and at complete odds with the dark promise in his eyes.

"Don't go easy on my account." I gasped as he filled me.

His hands slid beneath me to draw me closer to the edge of the bed, gripping my ass.

"You want it harder?"

He thrust inside of me. A loud moan ripped from my lips. He hit a sensitive spot with a quick twist and swivel of his hips. His powerful body reared over me, his eyes burning into me.

"You want it like this?" he asked.

He thrust again, and again, each thrust harder and more relentless than the last. Lust hummed in my veins as he pounded into me.

This was better than any fantasy. Better than my dream.

His mouth took hold of mine as he pumped between my thighs. Heat building, I lost the ability to breathe under the crushing weight of his body. We didn't make love. We fucked. We fucked like wild animals and lost ourselves in the pleasure. We were creatures meant to sin together, and revel in passion.

Born to rule.

When my next orgasm ripped through me, threatening to shatter my world, a random flash of inspiration struck me—was there a way to rule together?

I clung to him with my hands tangled in his hair as he continued his assault on my body, chasing his own orgasm. The world tilted on its axis until the final few thrusts of his hips told me he'd reached the edge.

Ryker pulled out at the last moment and spilled his seed on the sheets beside me.

I stared up, breathless, my limbs limp and my body satiated. A satisfied hum vibrated through my body. Would I ever recover from this?

"You—" I started, not quite sure what I planned to say, only that it was to accuse him of...something.

He swallowed my words with a kiss, and for a blissful moment, the rest of the world ceased to exist.

Unlike everything outside this room, I didn't doubt myself here. Ryker, on the other hand, knew how to do everything inside and outside the bedroom.

He was calm and collected under pressure. Strong and fearless when warranted.

How did I think I could rule?

Ryker got up and brought a towel over from my bathroom to help clean me up before pushing the soiled sheet aside.

"I can see you thinking," he said, his voice a rumbling growl.

Instead of spanking my ass and mumbling a thanks as he walked away, like I half-expected, Ryker settled beside me on the bed and drew me closer until he cocooned me, Big Spoon style.

"You're always thinking too much," he said.

"Would you say that's my only major flaw?" I asked, with only the barest note of teasing.

I felt him shake his head. "No. I'd say your biggest flaw is trying to take the throne."

"Well, well." I chuckled. "I could have bet money on you saying that."

"Sloane...you can do anything you want. I know you think you need the throne to survive, but you have the ability to do whatever you want, wherever you want. Why do you want this?"

I wanted to see his questions as a ploy, a way to keep me off-kilter so he could use it to his advantage, but I also wanted to think that we were past all that now.

Seemed I had a lot of wants, and not a lot of time to see them materialize.

"I'm sorry. I'm seeing this through to the end." I snuggled against him, wiggling my ass for emphasis. "I don't plan on dropping out."

"Well, good," he huffed into my ear. "I enjoy competing against you."

His admission might have surprised me if we

hadn't just fucked like rabid animals. Because honestly, that was the craziest thing I'd ever done in my life. Not because of how much I enjoyed it, but because he was my enemy, and I'd given him access to me in the most intimate way possible.

"Oh, shut up," I told him.

"Would you rather I lie to you?"

I'd rather he gave up the throne and tell me he needed me. Or that he wanted me as more than just a spur in his side to get him through the Inferno.

Yup, I had a whole lot of wants, and only time would tell if I ever saw them materialize.

CHAPTER TWENTY

I walked into the dining hall beside Ryker, and nothing happened. None of the conversations stopped. Dishes didn't fall to the stone floor with a clatter. No one even looked at us, too busy chatting and shoveling food into their faces.

But surely, they had to know. Surely, everyone knew or at least heard my world falling down around me and getting shattered.

I was confused.

My emotions were a mess, while my body hummed with vitality and an annoying warmth kept squeezing my chest every time my gaze settled on Ryker.

Surely, everyone knew.

Chupey brushed past me and headed for the area that provided food for familiars and left me to my jumbled thoughts. What the hell was I supposed to do now? Did Ryker and I move our separate ways? Is this when Ryker would reveal it was all an act? God, if he did that, I'd have to cock-punch him. And I'd grown rather fond of his junk.

It didn't seem like an act.

Everything certainly felt quite real this morning, especially when we decided to go another round in the sack before breaking for food.

"Come on." Ryker jerked his chin to the right. "This way."

He led me to a table where a familiar-looking demon sat with a platter of food in front of him.

"Slade, Sloane. You two know each other, right?" Ryker had many qualities, but making introductions wasn't one of them.

Slade froze with his fork halfway to his mouth, syrup dripping from the chunk of pancake. His gaze darted between the two of us. Instead of taking another mouthful of his breakfast, he set the fork down and swallowed. "I see things have...changed."

Ryker sat down on the bench across from his friend and patted the seat beside him.

"Uh..." Yeah, I didn't need a side of awkward with my pancakes.

"Sit down," Ryker said. "Slade won't bite."

No. Slade looked more like he'd rip the head from his enemies and roar over their twitching remains, but okay. I slipped onto the bench beside Ryker and sat quietly while Ryker loaded pancakes onto my plate from the main platter.

Pancakes.

In Hell.

Who knew?

Slade continued to stare at me. He reached for a glass of water and took a long drink. "You didn't strike me as the quiet type," he finally said.

"Still processing." And I was. Sitting next to Ryker, talking to him, sleeping with him, it all felt so natural and right, like I should've been doing this my whole adult life despite my initial reaction to despise everything about him.

I didn't want to go back to hating him, but we also still had to compete for the same prize. Neither one of us was going to back down. I wasn't the type to set aside my dreams for a man, and I wasn't about to start now.

"Yeah," Slade said. "Me, too."

Ryker grunted and ate with relaxed efficiency as if none of this bothered or concerned him at all. But he could only dodge his friend's questioning gaze for so long.

Ryker set his fork down and sighed. "Okay, go ahead and ask."

Slade's gaze slid to me.

"Real subtle," I muttered.

"You can ask in front of her," Ryker said, taking a sip of water.

"What does this mean?" Slade waved his finger between us.

"Well, this is awkward." Ryker leaned forward, resting his elbows on the table to clasp his hands over his plate. "I had hoped that new minx of a girlfriend you've been shacked up with helped you sort this out, but I'll try my best. When a man and a woman like each other, the man inserts his pe—"

"Stop." Slade shook his head. "You're such a dick."

I kind of agreed with Ryker's friend. I also wanted to know the answer to Slade's question.

Ryker grinned, flashing his teeth. "You asked."

"That's not what I asked, and you know it. What does this relationship mean? Do you still plan to compete? What's changed?"

Ryker leaned back and wiped his mouth with a napkin. "Nothing has changed. Sloane and I will still compete for the throne. I know my dick is magical, but I doubt it will deter her from her goal, nor will she knock me from my path. And when I win—"

"When I win," I interrupted him. "Ryker will already have experience getting on his knees for me."

Ryker laughed, really laughed, and I couldn't help but smile, too.

Maybe I didn't know exactly what was happening between me and Ryker, or what would happen to us in the future, but that was okay. We could figure it out as we went. As long as he wasn't a sore loser when I won, everything would be fine.

CHAPTER TWENTY-ONE

I stepped out of the swirling green haze of the fifth portal and caught my breath. For once, I wasn't sprawling face first in the dirt. The view in front of me was amazing.

No, not amazing. That sounded like rolling hills of wildflowers and sparkling sunlight dancing on blades of fresh grass. This view wasn't a Valentine's Day card filled with poetry. Not even close.

Blue-gray mist clung to the base of a jagged peaked mountain. A raging ocean crashed nearby, the sound breaking the silence. Above, a large moon cast silvery strands of light down on the dark forest encircling the area. But the eerie night scene wasn't what stole my breath away.

What amazed me was the sight immediately in front of me.

Two tall horse-like creatures loomed over me and

Ryker. Black as midnight, matching wings protruded from their backs. Plated armor covered their necks and the front of their heads, protecting the bridges of their noses and muzzles. They had the same shape and musculature as horses, even their head shape bore a similarity, but no one would ever mistake the creatures in front of me for horses.

Large, antler-like horns protruded from their heads. Directly below, bright, white-blue eyes glowed with intelligence. One of the creatures bobbed its head up and down and flashed its teeth.

Fangs.

"What are they?"

"Demon mounts." Ryker strode up to the one directly in front of him and held out his hand.

The demon mount leaned forward and snuffled his open palm. Without warning, it clamped onto Ryker's hand with its fangs.

"Ryker." I stepped forward.

He closed his eyes and shook his head.

The demon mount released his hand, blood running down his arm and dripping to the ground.

"A deal has been struck." Ryker opened his eyes and bolted into the saddle with ease.

Well, shit.

Ryker turned to me, flashing a large grin. "Worried about me, princess?"

I snorted and ignored the pitter-patter of my heart. I had been worried. Though we had finally given in to our more...*primal* needs, it felt like an awful lot more than just sex.

At least for me.

But I couldn't let these confusing feelings for Ryker prevent me from winning. I needed to live. He didn't *need* to see his vendetta through.

Of course, he wouldn't agree with this point. To him, his revenge was almost all-consuming.

Almost.

Not enough to prevent him from taking me to O-town.

Maybe there was a way to diffuse his rage. Maybe we could be something once I won the throne. Or maybe... Maybe we could share the throne, somehow.

"Hurry up, princess."

I hesitated before copying Ryker's actions. Something flashed in the demon mount's eyes, and it stepped forward. Its teeth sank into my palm, and I winced. There was nothing gentle about the bite.

My name is Wrathen, a scratchy voice spoke in my head.

Err...

I embraced my magic and tried to speak in my head. *My name is Sloane.*

I was a total idiot. Why would I think this would work?

Because it does, Wrathen answered me. *You need to control your thoughts, youngling. I can hear it all.*

I swallowed. I didn't envy the demon mount one bit. My head was not a fun place to be.

Wrathen snorted. Yeah, he must've caught that thought, too.

What exactly am I supposed to do? I asked.

We need to strike a deal.

I've never done this before.

I can tell, the demon mount's voice was dry and emotionless.

I'm sorry.

Don't be. I was your father's mount. It would be my honor to lead you through this trial. He brought his head up and down and fanned out his magnificent wings before folding them tightly against his back.

Is it a race then?

Yes, but the objective is not as it seems.

Will you tell me what the objective is? That would be a first—knowing what to expect.

The willowy council demon with green hair, brown skin and no horns had stood beside the portal this morning with a broad smile. Gwyn, the demon of the wild hunt. If they intended for us to hunt each other or some random creature, they didn't see it necessary to outfit us with weapons.

Identifying the purpose of this trial before it starts will not be a part of our deal.

What will be? I asked.

I will be your mount and you will be my rider. He stomped his feet to emphasize each word. Unlike the back two legs that ended in hooves that appeared made of shiny obsidian, his front two legs ended in paws. Much like any large carnivore, sharp claws protruded from those paws.

What does this entail? I asked

Our deal will be that l take care of you, and you will take care of me.

Ryker's mount pranced nearby, impatience in every step.

"It's not exactly rocket science, princess."

I squinted at Ryker before answering Wrathen. *We have a deal.*

The demon mount released my hand and I stepped to his side.

Growing up, we moved from place to place and lived paycheck to paycheck, and opportunities to learn how to ride a horse were non-existent. Adulthood and city living hadn't changed that.

Of course, I had done the fair stuff, where they plunked the kid-version of me on the saddle of a well-broke pony and led me around along the inside a fenced-in pen. But riding wouldn't appear on my list of skills.

Punching in faces, yes.

Riding, no.

I placed a foot in the stirrups and swung up into the saddle, careful to avoid the wings. Once seated, I wasn't in danger of crushing Wrathen's wings. They protruded just behind where my knees rested against his side.

Flank, he corrected.

Geez. He wasn't lying when he said he could hear all my thoughts.

I'm not an experienced rider, I told him.

Wrathen snorted again, and I didn't need to hear his voice in my head to know he agreed with my assessment.

"So graceful," Ryker noted. "Mesmerizing."

"Shut up." I turned to him. "What now?"

"We ride."

"To do what?" I waved at the forest. "What's the purpose of this trial?"

Ryker shrugged. "My demon mount wouldn't say. I suspect it's a race."

"Hardly seems fair." One of us had experience riding and it wasn't me. But, Wrathen had said this trial wasn't what it seemed. Maybe I still had a chance.

Time to go. Wrathen gave me a second of warning before he launched forward. I gripped the reins in one hand and the saddle with the other and held on for my life.

I didn't know a lot about horses or riding aside from the four gates—walk, trot, canter, and gallop. I used to get sucked into watching televised horse jumping events and cheered for the horse with the best name despite knowing absolutely nothing about the sport.

This demon mount didn't move like any of the

horses I'd seen. Wrathen went straight from standing to what must be a demon mount equivalent to a gallop. He didn't hesitate, he didn't ease into it, gradually getting faster. One moment, I sat in the saddle, ogling Ryker on his demon mount and then, after a moment of suspension, we hurtled through the dark forest.

His feet struck the ground. His front legs made no sound, while the back two made a similar sound to horses running. It sounded weird. It felt odd.

I wanted off.

Unease curled in my gut, and as I leaned forward, the familiar tickle of magic raced down my spine. Glancing around, pink ribbons of magic wrapped around us and crackled in my ears. It was binding us together, connecting me to Wrathen.

Something clicked then, and the pressure of the energy ceased. That's when Wrathen let out a high-pitched squeal of delight, one that I felt in my bones.

I had fused with the giant demon mount.

It was difficult to describe, but I could suddenly feel the earth flying underneath us as we sped past trees and thick brush. I sensed his rapid heartbeat—felt it as if it pounded next to my own. I could count his breaths, match them to mine. We were moving as if we were one.

Holy shit. This is terrifying.

Ryker moved his mount closer, a large grin on his face. I didn't need to ask. He loved every minute of this.

His mount strained forward, his head bobbing with each powerful stride, his pointed teeth flashing just as brightly as Ryker's.

We raced on beside each other, time seeming to stand still to allow us some freedom. I glanced over at Ryker again. If only we could stay like this. If only life was as simple as riding demon mounts through the forest together.

After what felt like an hour, Wrathen's breathing became ragged.

Are you okay?

I'm fine.

Foam frothed from the mouth of Ryker's mount, and his coat glistened with sweat.

Neither of you look fine, I said. *Is this normal for you? To run for so long at this speed?*

No.

We broke free of the forest. A small village appeared out of the mist. Firelight illuminated a few windows, but darkness drenched the majority of the town. A tall stone wall surrounded the buildings.

"What are those?" I asked.

Large furry-shaped beasts ran around the outside of the town, howling, snarling and throwing themselves at the town wall.

"Werewolves." Ryker pressed his lips together and spurred his mount forward.

This is what Wrathen meant. This trial wasn't

about a race, it was about the village and these werewolves.

Wrathen grunted and followed. As we closed the distance, more prickles of power, more magic, and I watched as silver-plated armor materialized over my chest, shoulders, and thighs.

"What the f—" But before I could ever finish the sentence, a long sword appeared in my hand, just like the daggers had when I'd faced Borca in the colosseum sand trial.

Okay, this was fucking cool. I was like some Hellish version of *Xena: Warrior Princess*.

The moment of glory was short lived when I realized Wrathen struggled underneath me. He was tapped, and sympathy had me rethinking this entire thing. He might be a ferocious mount, but he'd likely keel over if I took him into battle.

Stop, I instructed him.

What? Why?

I tugged on the reins to let him know I was serious, and he slowed enough for me to swing my leg over the saddle and hop off. Instantly, the invisible bond between us broke. All my sensations and thoughts became my own again. And a sense of loss washed over me.

What are you doing? he asked.

You've done enough for me, I said. *You need to rest.*

He tosses his head side to side. *I can do this.*

I won't be responsible for you passing out from

exhaustion. I patted his neck for reassurance. *Thank you for bringing me this far.*

A howl ripped through the air, and my blood turned into ice in my veins.

That couldn't be good...

"Shit, some of them spotted us!" Ryker and his mount blew past us toward the village. To my horror, a dozen monstrous wolf creatures sped toward us. Now dressed in golden armor and holding a sword himself, Ryker wasted no time launching him and his mount at the nearest werewolf. His blade cut through the beast easily, but as one went down, two more surged forward.

"Listen," I blurted out loud out of habit. The beasts rushed for me and Wrathen, making my words a jumbled mess. "Run from here. Get yourself somewhere safe!"

When one of the werewolves got too close, I lashed out my sword. It leaped away and then came for me again, but this time, I faked left and managed to stab the thing in the chest. Right where the heart should be.

I glanced over my shoulder to find Wrathen still hadn't moved.

Gripping my sword firmly, I slashed down another wolf but wasn't quick enough to stop another from raking its claws across my breastplate, piercing through the metal.

Thinking fast, I whipped out the weapon and sliced off its arm. Blood sprayed over me and all over the ground. The werewolf yipped in pain and retreated.

Heart thundering, I took a second to examine my damaged armor. Luckily, the creature's talons hadn't reached my skin, but it had definitely been too close for comfort.

Another wolf snarled behind me. By the time I whirled around, its blazing yellow eyes and open snout with sharp teeth barreling down on me. My stomach plummeted. I had no time to scream.

A blur of darkness jutted out from my right and suddenly the werewolf was hit and thrown sideways, away from me. At first, I thought it might be Ryker again, but when I saw Wrathen's dark coat shining in the moonlight, I realized he had kicked the creature with his powerful back legs.

As the werewolf rolled away from us, I hurried over, held up my sword, and plunged the blade into the beast's chest until it stopped moving.

Wrathen trotted over to me, and I reached out to pat his wet, matted fur. *Thank you, friend.*

He ducked his head down and butted it against mine.

A werewolf screeched in agony in the distance. Its blood-curdling death cry raised every hair on my body. Ryker and his mount must've taken another one down.

We work together, Wrathen said.

I nodded, understanding. *I take care of you.*

And I take care of you.

Together, we turned and ran toward the remaining werewolves. I hacked and cut down any of the beasts that dared come at me, while Wrathen bucked and kicked and used his wings to knock the others off their feet. With Ryker and his mount working in the distance, it wasn't long before we defeated all the wolves as a team.

I was covered in blood.

Again.

This was becoming a weird-ass habit of mine, wasn't it?

When everything was quiet, I searched the area for Ryker and saw him and the tailend of his mount disappearing around the town's wall, probably searching for any stragglers.

Oh God. Could there be more?

Another guttural howl piercing the silence confirmed those fears.

Sloane, Wrathen's voice ripped my attention away from Ryker and the werewolves.

I turned toward him.

You will make a fine leader someday.

My chest warmed. *Thank you.*

He dipped his head again.

Just then, a portal snapped open a few feet away.

I hesitated.

Wait, was the trial over? But not all the werewolves were defeated. The town wasn't saved.

Did that mean I'd failed?

Wrathen snorted. *Sloane, this trial tested empathy, ruthlessness, and keeping your word. Our deal was fulfilled. By showing me kindness, you demonstrated empathy. Empathy is not a weakness, but know that sometimes ruthlessness is also needed.*

I glanced over my shoulder to where I last saw Ryker.

Wrathen bobbed his head. *That one proved his ruthless side. He did not care about his mount's health or safety. Only victory. But that was their deal.*

I rolled my eyes. Of course, it was.

The village faded away, leaving a mist-covered field, a few wildflowers glowing under the moonlight.

Watch out for that one, Wrathen answered.

I reached out and scratched his muzzle.

Oh, I intend to.

CHAPTER TWENTY-TWO

After Wrathen's warning, I knew I shouldn't be with Ryker again. I especially shouldn't be letting him touch me the way he was. But I couldn't help it.

Was I an idiot?

Probably.

Was I going to regret this soon?

Without a fucking doubt.

But for reasons I couldn't understand, being with him was like a drug for me and I couldn't stop getting high on him—his closeness, his touch, and the way he tasted...

I was doomed.

So, instead of dwelling on the impending catastrophe of my love life, I watched Ryker move between my thighs and make my world shatter into small pieces.

I watched him lick and kiss and nip my sensitive skin. I watched him worship my body.

And when my mind was dizzy with pleasure, my lust sated and my body content, I watched him still.

He was beautiful.

And he would destroy me.

Ryker would be my downfall, but I couldn't pull myself away.

"You're lost in thought." Ryker ran his fingers down my arm. We lay in my bed, Ryker on his back and me half-sprawled over him. The sweat sticking us together had cooled but my body still tingled from the aftermath of multiple orgasms.

If I made Ryker feel half as good as he made me feel, I was a fucking goddess.

"Just thinking about things," I said.

Ryker snorted and let his hand fall away from my arm. "That was my point."

"You mean you want to know what I'm thinking?"

"Of course."

"Isn't that my line?"

Ryker chuckled, his chest rumbling under my cheek.

I trailed my fingers down his strong chest, swirling patterns along his skin. "I was wondering how it's possible to hate and yet equally like someone."

"Do you truly hate me?" He didn't sound offended. More curious, if anything.

"No. At least not anymore. When you ordered me to be your coffee table, I definitely hated you."

He rubbed the stubble on his chin. "That was one of my more ingenious moments."

"More deplorable, you mean."

"I'm sorry I asked—"

"Ordered." I lifted my head to glare at him.

"Ordered," he acknowledged with a dip of his chin. "I'm sorry I ordered you to be my coffee table. I might've gotten a little carried away and I liked seeing you on your hands and knees like that."

"Thank you. For the apology, not for being a dirty pervert."

"You really should thank me for that as well."

My cheeks warmed, but I ignored his comment and rested my head back on his chest to resume drawing swirling patterns with my fingers. "Have you thought about what you'll do after the Inferno?"

"Not really. I imagine I'll be busy running the Underworld." He dropped a kiss on the top of my head. "Don't worry. I'll still have time for you. Hell, if Slade can make it work with a mortal, I'm sure we can sort something out."

I shook my head, momentarily derailed from my point. "Slade's girlfriend is a mortal?"

"Yeah. It's a long story. I'll let him tell you when you see him next. But the point is, you don't need to worry. Things don't need to change between us when I become Lucifer."

Arrogant bastard. Why did I find his attitude so appealing? "Have you thought about what you'll do when I win?"

"No."

"Why not?"

"Why waste time worrying over something unlikely to occur?" His chest rumbled. He was fucking with me now. Though I knew he believed he'd win and had the stronger claim, I also knew he'd never discounted me as a competitor. At least not after the first trial. He had to have thought about a contingency plan.

"Am I going to have to worry about you organizing an uprising once I win, or can we continue seeing each other like this?" I asked.

"I don't see why one would preclude the other."

Now he really was messing with me.

"No, Sloane." He gathered me in his arms and squeezed. "If you win, I will accept my defeat. You won't have to worry about me."

His unspoken words hung heavy in the room. "Just the rest of the Underworld?"

"Pretty much."

CHAPTER TWENTY-THREE

The swirling black and gray mist of the final portal beckoned me like a cold lace of frost skittering over autumn leaves. Beautiful, delicate, intoxicating in a strange way.

I should run in the opposite direction.

My hindsight rang in my head. Whatever waited for me on the other side wasn't safe. I'd lose a piece of myself once I stepped through the swirling mists, and the life I knew would be forfeit in one way or another.

With only the two of us left in the competition, Ryker stood solemnly and silently at my side. He stared straight ahead unblinking. Although I thought I saw a hint of hesitation on his part too, I knew better than to think it would change anything. Ryker wouldn't back down and neither would I.

Chupey leaned against my leg in support. "Don't be nervous," he told me.

"Do I look it?" I asked him.

"It's the final trial. Keep going, Sloane. You're almost there," he said. "You'll have your life back."

Ryker visibly shook himself and glanced down at my familiar. He opened his mouth to say something, but the council members stepped forward.

"It's time," Moloch said. "May the best demon win."

Without another word, Ryker and I stepped forward through the swirling darkness in tandem and thankfully I didn't fall flat on my face. Apparently, embracing my demon nature and unlocking all my magic had some perks.

Ryker walked ahead as I adjusted to the change in lighting.

Wearing my tank top, shorts, and a sturdy pair of boots, I stepped onto a wide circular platform that seemed to hang in the darkness with nothing anchoring it in space. I glanced around to survey my surroundings, but the mist made of shadows hid anything and everything beyond the hard, stone platform I stood on. Even the air gave nothing away–no smell, no wind. This place felt like a frozen moment in time and place.

"Ryker?" I called out, listening to the strange way my voice echoed back to me. He'd walked into those shadows, and I lost sight of him.

Slowly, the reverberating sound of footsteps grew louder as a shape disengaged from the darkness.

Ryker.

With a fucking sword in his hand and a guilty expression.

"What are you doing?" I asked.

But I knew. I knew in that instant what the last trial meant and what was expected of us.

This trial, courtesy of the last demon, Moloch, would pit us against one another. A fight to the death with the winner taking the throne.

I shook my head as Ryker stepped closer. I didn't have a weapon. I swallowed over the rapidly growing lump in my throat. My mouth had gone dry, and it felt like acid ran inside my veins instead of blood. I reached for my magic, the same magic that let me bond with Wrathen, form portals, and fight like a beast against werewolves. The power surged up and the same sword from the last trial materialized in my hand.

I glanced down at the weapon and then back at Ryker. "I don't want to do this."

"You knew this was how things would end," Ryker finally said, regret laced in those words.

"I guess I did." I slowly circled around him, keeping him in my sights at all times.

Yes, I'd known deep in my gut we headed toward a face-off, but I had hoped for a different ending, a better solution. We had talked about continuing our relationship after the Inferno, but we had been lying to ourselves.

Mom always said to hope for the best, and plan for

the worst, and I hadn't forgotten that motto. I had no intention of dying today.

My attention fractured between Ryker and the edge of the platform. I didn't want to know what would happen if I fell over the side.

I'd probably fall for eternity.

"I don't want to fight you, Sloane," Ryker said.

"That sword in your hand says otherwise. Why don't you put it down and we can talk?"

Ryker glanced at the steel blade he held, and his grip tightened. Yeah, I didn't think so. I refused to let him back me into a position where I had to fight him. As great as my demon magic made me fight, I'd seen Ryker in action. He didn't suffer the mistakes that came from being stuck on the beginning portion of the learning curve. He could—and would—cut me down.

The thought caused a wave of revulsion to crash through me, to the point where I had to swallow down the heat.

Fight him? Kill him? After everything we'd been through, I'd rather chop off my own leg. Although I wouldn't go so far as to throw myself over the side of the platform, either.

There had to be another way out of this.

"The trial won't end until one of us is dead," Ryker told me. His gaze pierced through my skin straight down to the core of me.

"I can stand here for a long time," I said.

"You're seriously not going to make a move?" he asked.

I arched my brow. "Should I?"

"That is literally the whole point," Ryker snapped. "Come on. We have to do this. You have to come for me."

He lurched forward and I responded by pivoting to the right, keeping him directly in front of me. He hadn't even tried with that lunge.

He growled in frustration.

"You understand why, don't you?" he continued, arching his shoulders forward in an almost menacing air.

And I did. He wanted to win but couldn't bring himself to attack me. He could cut me down to defend himself, he could justify my death then, but as long as I remained inactive, he couldn't bring himself to do it. Right now, Ryker battled his own morals more than he did me.

I pulled back and banished my sword. "You can try to fight me if you want, Ryker, but I'm not doing it. I'm not moving against you."

"Why?"

"Because I don't want to hurt you. I can't hurt you. If winning this trial means killing you, then I'm stepping aside for you to rule." I hadn't meant to say that, hadn't meant to say any of it, but as soon as the words left my mouth, the truth in them sent warmth spreading across my chest.

The decision cost me nothing and everything at the same time. I'd made my choice the moment I saw him stalk toward me.

"You win." I held my hands up in front of me to show my willingness to give up. No hesitation, not anymore. Rightness settled inside of me at my decision. "It's yours."

"It's not that I don't want it, Sloane, because you know I do." His voice trailed off and he gripped his sword, still refusing to let it go.

I bit down on my bottom lip to keep the tears threatening to fall from doing so. They burned the corners of my eyes, like the acid in my veins was spilling out at long last.

"I'm backing out, Ryker. Don't you understand? If it means killing you, then—"

"What?" he interrupted. "Then what?"

"You tell me," I said.

"I want the throne...but not like this," Ryker shook his head. "Never like this. Not when it means losing you, too."

"Those are pretty words, but I don't believe you mean them. But it doesn't matter. I know how I feel and, for the first time in a long time, I know what I have to do."

He glanced toward the edge of the platform and his eyes grew wide. "You wouldn't."

Maybe it really was the mind control. Maybe he'd

influenced my feelings to the point where I'd do anything for him.

At this point, I didn't care how I developed these feelings. I only knew that I had them. I had them and I cherished them, and I meant every word I said.

My fingers itched to place my hand on his cheek and wipe away the confusion on his face. That wasn't how things would end between us, though.

"Either I win, and you die, or you win, and I die," Ryker said, his usual growl cracking.

I shook my head. "I choose a third option."

Gathering my power, I centered it in my core, stoking the fire and waiting for it to build, to grow and change and consume the whole of me until that sense of rightness clicked into place. Then, harnessing the demon magic in my palms, I raised them in the murky air in front of me.

I can do this.

It was my gift, wasn't it? My birthright, thanks to the father I'd never known. Did I even have to spill my blood, draw a rune or use an incantation?

Time to find out.

I sent the power outward and watched as a dime-sized ball of light appeared in the gloom. The light grew until a portal large enough for me to step through loomed in front of me, vibrating with magic.

"Sloane, don't do this. Don't run away," Ryker called out from behind me.

It wasn't running away. At least, it wasn't in my mind. I found the only available option left to me that didn't involve death.

At least, not more death.

Hadn't I seen enough of it?

The glow of the portal caressed my skin and I hesitated again. A love sacrifice. Never in a million years could I have foreseen this.

"I'm sorry," I called back to him.

Then I stepped forward into the mortal realm. Prepared to live out whatever days were left to me.

Alone.

Because that seemed like a better alternative than anything the last trial offered. If I had stayed to face Ryker in battle, I'd likely lose, and now that I was back in the mortal realm, I faced death anyway. But this way, I had a choice. And this choice meant Ryker wouldn't have to live with killing me to gain the throne. At least I could give him that—a clear conscience.

Ryker would make a good leader. He'd already proven that. The glow of magic died behind me, leaving me standing alone in my apartment.

After facing those horrific trials, I no longer feared my disease, but living without the man I'd fallen for seemed like the worst kind of punishment.

I took a deep breath and looked at my apartment. It appeared untouched and exactly the same as I had left it, including the smear of blood on my living room floor. Had Becca come over that night? Had she used her key to find me gone with my blood all over? I winced. I needed to see her and make things right before my time was up.

I had made a choice.

And now I had to live with it.

CHAPTER TWENTY-FOUR

I had gone over what I planned to say to Becca at least a hundred times on my way to her place, but after knocking, every one of my so-called explanations evaporated into dust. She swung the door open, and when her blazing gaze settled on me, my mouth dried.

Oh shit. She was *pissed*.

She rocked back on her heels. "Oh, I'm sorry. Who are you?"

"Cut it out, Becca." I stepped forward, but my friend didn't budge from the doorway. "You saw me through the peephole."

Becca folded her arms over her chest. "Maybe. I dunno. You kind of look like a friend I had once, a long time ago, but it's hard to tell."

I'd been gone for maybe a week, two tops. Time

might flow differently between the two realms, but not *that* differently.

I held my arms out to my sides, hands open. "I'm sorry Becca. Some things came up—"

Becca shook her head, slow at first until she vibrated with visible anger. "No. No, you do not get to go missing, you do not get to ignore my calls, you do not get to leave blood smeared all over your floor so when I finally do stomp across town and use your spare key, I get to worry that you're fucking dead. You don't get to do any of that and then magically grace my doorstep with a pathetic apology."

Err. I didn't really have a plan aside from saying sorry. My heart was still shattered from walking away from the Immortal Throne and Ryker, and I could only cry on Chupey's shoulder for so long—if he ever forgave me and came back to live with me again.

I wouldn't blame him for wanting to stay in the Underworld. It was his true home, after all. His absence had left me empty. I wanted and needed a friend. Even if it was a human friend. But after that speech, I wondered if I still had one. I wasn't exactly best friend material.

"Can I come in and explain?" I asked. I'd probably scare the crap out of her, and she might try to get me committed, but at least she'd have the truth. If she didn't want to be friends after this, then I'd have to walk away and accept her decision.

Maybe Zane would come visit me with some of

that demonic brew we got wasted on. I'd give anything for one of his god-awful dad jokes right now.

She hesitated and glanced over her shoulder. "I have company."

"The new guy? I really would like to meet him."

Becca sighed and stepped back, opening up a space for me to enter her home. I didn't pause or give her time to second guess her decision. I needed to make up for being an asshole bestie and I'd start with making a good impression with her latest sugar daddy.

"Babe, where did you say the—" A familiar voice cut off as a man walked into the foyer.

With long hair and a half-shaven head, broad shoulders and an impish grin, the only thing different about Slade's appearance were the bullshit blue contacts he wore to dull the impact of his piercing gaze, and the lack of horns. They must disappear in the mortal realm, just as my hair returned to its dull brown color.

Slade froze mid-step, his mouth dropping open.

"You!" I lunged forward. Gathering my magic around me, I slammed him against the wall, holding him in place with my forearm pressed into his neck. He didn't fight back, didn't even try, but with the amount of power singing in my rage-filled veins, he wouldn't have succeeded.

"Sloane," Becca screeched somewhere behind me.

"What are you doing here?" I asked Slade.

Becca gripped my shoulders and tried to pull me

away from the demon. I didn't budge. Instead, I leaned forward and placed more pressure on his throat.

"You guys haven't taken enough from me? You have to take my friend as well?"

Slade didn't answer. Fury sparked in his gaze, but my power held him immobile while I slowly choked him.

Becca shook me, a hysterical sob ripping from her lips. "Let him go."

"He's not who you think he is," I snapped over my shoulder. "He's not *what* you think he is."

"I know, Sloane," she said. "I know."

"I highly doubt it."

"He's a demon," she said.

I snapped my head to the side, finally breaking my stare-down with Slade. I released the pressure from his neck but held him in place with my magic. "Wh... what? How do you know that?" Becca wasn't a supernatural being. She was as human as they came.

"He told me." Becca's gaze darted between me and the demon. "What I'd like to know is how you knew."

I pulled back my power and stepped away from Slade. Before he moved, I jabbed my finger into his chest. "If you try anything, if you try to hurt her, I'll end you."

Slade swallowed and nodded. "I know."

"I can do it," I said.

"I know." He licked his lips and swallowed. "Only truly powerful demons, like Lucifer, can manifest power like you just did in the mortal realm. I'm good, but not that good. Not good enough to take on a pissed off Dazamon."

"*I know,*" I mocked. I hadn't actually known any of that, but he had to be mistaken because I sure as hell didn't win the crown.

"Well, apparently I don't know shit." Becca placed her hand on a cocked hip. "So, someone better start explaining."

We awkwardly navigated to her small living room, and I stared down Slade while Becca grabbed us all beers.

"Here you go." Becca placed a cold bottle of beer on the coffee table in front of me before walking over to sit beside Slade on the loveseat. His hand slid over her knee, and he thanked her before plucking one of the bottles from her hand.

I blinked.

Slade and Becca remained on the couch, a perfect picture of domestic bliss.

"I really need you to explain this to me, Slade." I waved my hand between the two of them in case there was any doubt.

"Nuh uh." Becca shook her head. "You first. I'm the one missing the most information."

"Well, first I need to..." I cleared my throat and glared at Slade. "I kind of wanted to have this conversation in private. You know...just the two of us."

"Tough." Becca slid her hand onto Slade's thigh.

Gross. "Okay. Well, I need to apologize. I realize I've been a pretty poor friend, not just over the last few weeks, but for a while. I haven't been there for you, but expected you to always be there for me, and I'm sorry."

Her expression softened. "You lost your mom, Sloane."

I swallowed and looked away. "I know, but that doesn't make it okay. I'm sorry and I want to be a better friend."

"Like, be on time?"

I winced. "Like, try my best to be more on time."

Becca snorted.

"And listen to you and pay more attention to the things that are important to you." I only had a month or so left to live, and I had to make it count.

"Okay..." Becca glanced at Slade. "Right now, what's important to me is to understand what's going on. Where have you been? How did you know Slade was a demon? How did you just pin a two-hundred-pound block of demon muscle to my hallway wall without breaking a sweat?"

"It's a long story," I hedged.

"Good thing I have time and a whole fridge full of beer," she said.

Turned out, my story took three beers and less than an hour. I outlined everything that had happened since I met Ryker, leaving nothing out. It helped that Becca had already accepted the existence of demons. She didn't need time to process that specific aspect of my story.

While I spoke, Becca moved to sit beside me and when I finally got to the end and described my sacrifice, she reached out and rubbed my shoulders.

"So, after all that, you lost?" she whispered.

"Yeah."

"I'm really proud of you," Becca said.

"Huh?" I finally looked up at her.

She pulled back, dropping her hands to her lap, her eyes suspiciously watery. God, she better not cry. I hated when she did that.

"I'm proud of you," she repeated. "You went into this Inferno with no prior knowledge, with no one backing your corner—"

"Besides Chupey."

"Besides Chupey," she said. "And you almost won."

"Almost is the key word there. They don't give out participation ribbons, and the consolation prize is life back on earth and the same death sentence I had before I left." I spoke into my empty beer bottle.

Slade shifted on the couch across from us. He looked uncomfortable. We were demonstrating a lot of emotion, it probably conflicted with his evil demon soul.

If he had a soul.

I narrowed my eyes at him. "Now it's your turn, Slade. What are you doing here?"

He straightened in his seat. He might still look relaxed to someone like Becca, but to me he looked cautious, tense, ready to spring from his seat if I lunged for him.

"Ryker sent me to spy on Becca," he started. "To learn about the one person important in your life to potentially use against you, if needed."

I already wanted to lunge for him and punch him in the throat.

Becca pursed her lips. Had he told her this part or was she learning this for the first time, too?

"At first, I was supposed to keep my distance, but when one of her dates got handsy, I intervened," Slade continued.

I jerked upright and turned to Becca. "What? What date? Who was it? Why didn't you tell me?"

Becca scowled. "Well, Slade took care of him, so the guy didn't need immediate attention and I planned to tell you at lunch, but then you told me you were dying, and it hardly felt like the appropriate time. And then you disappeared, so stop glaring at me like that."

Crap. I settled back and tried to untwist my mouth. "Fair. Go on, Slade."

"And that's really all there was to it. Once we met, I couldn't stay away, even after Ryker told me to."

"Would you still have gone through with it?" I asked.

"With what?" He cocked his head, his long hair falling over his shoulders.

"If Ryker wanted to use her against me, would you have let him? Would you have helped him?"

Becca sucked in a breath.

Slade's gaze flashed, showing the demon lurking behind the contacts. "No. I wouldn't have, nor would he have asked after he realized she's mine. He's not a bad guy, you know."

For a demon. I snorted and placed my empty bottle on the coffee table. From the heated looks passing between Becca and Slade, I was overstaying my welcome.

I glanced at the coffee table. Would I have time to help Becca clean up before they jumped each other, or should I just make a hasty retreat now?

"Don't you want to know how Ryker is doing?" Slade asked.

I did. Oh, I fucking did. And sitting a few feet away from me, his bestie had all the answers. But I couldn't bring myself to ask, I couldn't open myself up to the possibility of hope and more potential hurt.

"No," I said, and chose the hasty retreat.

CHAPTER TWENTY-FIVE

"When are you going to stop moping?"

I glanced over at Chupey from my position at the window, chin resting on my palm and my elbow balanced on the sill. I lifted an eyebrow at the snarky tone. "Since when do you care whether I mope? You've gotten your walkies today."

Chupey panted, his tongue lolling out of the side of his mouth. "I'm just saying that being heartbroken isn't a good look for you."

This was what life looked like for me now. Back in the cage, back to doing what I excelled at, and for what? To come home alone to a demon familiar who constantly berated me for what I did. It wasn't so much that he disapproved, only that he wished my emotions would stop making the decisions for me.

When he'd returned from the Underworld, I'd held

him and cried, but our dynamic quickly returned to our familiar bickering.

"He wasn't going to kill you, you know," Chupey continued.

"Stop trying to make me feel better." I cast him some serious side-eye. This wasn't the first time he'd tried but for some reason, his insistence irritated me today.

"He wasn't," Chupey continued. "I saw the way he looked at you. I heard how he broke Mobius's hands because he dared to touch you. Those aren't the actions of an indifferent man."

"It doesn't matter now," I tossed back to him, rising at last to grab my bag. I'd wasted enough time. The fights wouldn't wait for me.

"But it does matter. He didn't do what you think he did, Sloane." Chupey trotted after me on the way to the door.

And I really didn't want to hear it. Ryker and the Underworld no longer concerned me. "If you keep this up, I'm going to call that no-kill shelter."

This is it. I closed the door behind me, shutting my demon familiar inside the apartment and heading toward my next fight. *This is my life now.*

This was how every day would look until I died or actively made an effort to change, and that might be a long time coming.

How wonderful.

My opponent attempted to jam his fist against my teeth with all the force at his disposal. I dodged the swipe and kicked his leg out from underneath him. He'd been expecting the move but that didn't make it any less potent, and the beefy brawler stumbled back a step. Getting him off balance was good enough for me and I launched into an attack of my own.

The fights had been this way since I got back.

I thought they'd be harder than they actually were, considering my demon half was slowly killing me.

Except, for some reason, I didn't feel like I was knocking on death's door anymore and my demon magic continued to hum inside me.

"Fucking bitch." The guy looked up from a crouch and spat out some blood. "You were supposed to go down easily."

I approached him with a cocky saunter I'd learned to perfect over the years.

No, I didn't feel like death anymore. I felt good.

Better than I deserved to feel under the circumstances.

"Didn't they tell you?" I asked him, having to raise my voice over the jeers of the crowd gathered around the cage. "I have a reputation."

"You're a woman," the bald-headed asshole retorted.

"Ah, that's your mistake right there."

He launched out of the crouch and came at me with all of his strength, his growl rivaling the crowd in volume. I sidestepped him easily, spun, and slammed my fist into the back of his head, sending him sprawling forward. He landed on his stomach with a slap.

"I'm so much more than a woman."

The man scrambled to his feet. He should've stayed down. The demon inside of me rose to attention. The powers I'd claimed when I fought the monster during the tactical trial roared to life, and I embraced them wholeheartedly.

At once my magic clicked into place and I finished the match with a roundhouse kick, sending the man flying across the cage and into unconsciousness.

Realization smacked me in the head.

Why hadn't I seen it before?

The reason I no longer felt sick.

The reason I was doing better than before in the ring.

I'd embraced my demon self, which took death off the table. At least in terms of my "disease."

I laughed as two guards entered the cage and came to drag the guy away. I wasn't done, not yet. Lifting my hands in the air brought another round of cheering from those who watched, and when a second man entered the cage to take the place of the first, I beat the crap out of him too. My muscles were loose and limber but far from exhausted.

Shaking out my arms, I bounced from foot to foot, craning my neck first to one side, then the other.

Ready. Waiting.

Prepared to kick some more ass.

I felt good.

And I also felt so empty.

What was the point? I threw the first punch at my new opponent. What was the point of having an endless life if I had to spend it alone? Just me and Chupey, forever.

I loved my familiar, of course, but an eternity alone with him and his farts...

I wanted more.

I wanted...

I bit back the emotions, shaking away the daunting feelings. I could break down later. Right now, I'd revel in knowing death no longer waited for me.

I hadn't needed the throne to embrace my demon self. Maybe under normal circumstances I would've had to plunk my ass down on those royal cushions, but I'd negated the need to do so that moment during the Borca trial when I broke through whatever held my demon self separate.

The guy circling me in the cage squinted at me like I was insane. And maybe I was. I downed him with a punch-kick combo that sent him sprawling on his back.

One after another, I kicked the crap out of whoever

thought to stand in front of me. Normally, when entering the cage, we weren't allowed to do back-to-back fights. The organizers didn't like to exhaust the winners.

But soon they stopped trying to get me out. I waved away each attempt to call me out of the cage until finally they ended their efforts and simply let me do my thing.

Greg, the bookie, looked positively gleeful.

Finally, a lull settled over the Underground. It seemed even the crowd had finally had enough of me.

"Come on," I called out, waving my arms to get someone, anyone, to come forward. "Fight me. Fight me!"

Chest heaving, my breath caught, but I was nowhere near done. This was what I had left. An endless string of faces to pound and a reputation unmatched by anyone else.

For the longest time, no one came forward. The announcer droned on overhead, going over my stats for the day, and when I looked out at the crowd I saw something surprising.

Sympathy.

Well, greed and sympathy. A lot of people made a lot of money on me tonight, but others actually felt sorry for me.

Was that what I'd become?

I didn't have a chance to go down that road because someone in a hooded sweatshirt stepped through the gate and into the cage, just as the announcer called out for my final opponent.

"Just so we're clear." He lifted his head, revealing fierce—yet familiar—green eyes. "I bet against you, princess."

CHAPTER TWENTY-SIX

I stared at Ryker with my mouth opening and closing, but no sound coming out. It was pathetic, the way my heart skipped a beat and tried to tear itself out of my chest to get close to him.

Clearing my throat, I adjusted my stance so that I balanced on the balls of my feet. "That was a bad move," I replied. "Because I've been on a winning streak for ages."

Ryker shook his head and shifted so he mimicked my posture, his hands in front of him, his knees slightly bent. His jeans and T-shirt told me he hadn't come here to fight.

Well, he shouldn't have stepped into the cage with me.

The crowd remained silent, watching and listening. It wouldn't take them long to figure out we knew each other.

I raked my gaze over him, over all of those familiar lines and angles, over his gorgeous green eyes and the strong breadth of his shoulders.

Should I tell him I missed him? Should I tell him my life was dull without him, or that I dreamed about our ride through the forest on the demon mounts every night?

Absolutely not.

I hadn't realized how badly I wanted to see him until he stood in front of me. I made the first move before I thought about it, rushing at him and automatically putting him on the defensive. Of course, he managed to block every hit I threw his way. And I hit harder and harder. And with each blow, he dodged. Yet, he refused to hit back.

"I thought you said you put money on yourself?" I asked breathlessly. Perspiration beaded along my forehead for the first time today as we danced around each other. "This is no way to win."

"I actually thought we'd have a chance to talk to each other first," he told me, his face a severe mask I hadn't seen on him in a long time. "I forgot how bloodthirsty you are."

My heart thumped painfully once again. "If you wanted to talk, you should've asked me out, not stepped into a cage in an illegal fighting operation."

He hadn't reached out to me since I ripped a portal through the final trial of the Inferno to escape to the mortal realm. Not once.

Probably too busy ruling the Underworld.

So, what was he doing here? Why now?

"I'm pretty sure you would've turned me down." Ryker said.

"Got that right." I kicked out with my leg to try and bring him down, but the hit bounced off of his thigh and sent me back a step instead. I flashed my teeth.

"Come on. We're not here to talk," I snapped out.

Ryker lunged forward, lightning fast. My ass hit the canvas a second later, and Ryker loomed over me with his arms on either side of my head. His attention focused squarely on my mouth. At once, heat blossomed through me and I forgot about all the aches and pains from the day. I forgot about everything except for the feel of him and the way he fit snugly between my legs. Even the booing crowd faded away.

"Sloane," he said, my name a whisper in the wind and made goosebumps rise along my skin. "Do you have any idea how badly I've missed you?"

I shook my head. "You haven't missed me. This is... this is your mind control. You're doing this to me."

"When are you going to realize the truth? I have no control over you," he said. "I barely have control over myself when I'm with you."

"Bullshit," I spat.

He had the nerve to look affronted. "I'm serious. I can't control you with my touch and I never have. My powers don't work on you."

"Your powers seemed to work on me just fine when you helped me access my magic in the kitchen."

"That only worked because you wanted me to help. My magic can't force you to do anything you don't already want to do. You're stronger than me. You're a Dazamon."

I shook my head. "I don't believe you."

He made no move to get up as he asked, "Why?"

"Because you're a liar and you've been out for me from the start."

"I didn't realize you had such a poor opinion of me." He chuckled low and dipped his head down to the crook of my neck. His breath fanned the sensitive skin there. "And here I'd hoped for a warm welcome."

"You brought this on yourself, Ryker."

At last, he shifted back, rising and holding out a hand to help me to my feet. I took the help but dropped his hand as soon as possible to make a point. What point, however, I didn't know. I missed the feel of him instantly.

"I'm telling you the truth. I've never been able to control you," Ryker said, expression serious. "Your reactions are your own, just like mine belong to me. I can't help the way I feel about you."

He had no idea how badly I wanted to hear that from him, and the anger flashing in his gaze told me he wasn't saying these things to get a rise out of me. No... he meant them.

And that scared me.

"You hated me."

He shook his head. "I watched you for months. I wanted to despise you, and I did hate you. But not for the reasons you think."

I licked my lips, not quite ready to ask him what he meant by that. "You, ah, better go collect your winnings." I tucked a lock of sweat-slicked hair behind my ear. "You took me by surprise, and I suspect you cheated, but you beat me."

A slow smile spread across his face. "I'm here for a compromise, not for victory."

"What do you mean?"

Ryker took a slow step forward, then another.

I was in his arms a moment later and staring up, up, up into those flashing green eyes.

"Hear me out," he started.

"Well, we can't exactly discuss things in front of all these people, can we?"

His touch had me coming unhinged in the worst possible way. Or maybe the best. I didn't know anymore, because seeing him here threw me for a gigantic loop.

He hesitated and let me go, turning his glare to the crowd like it was their fault they existed.

I snorted and led the way out of the cage and into the locker room of the Underground. The crowd parted easily for Ryker. There was something about his presence that commanded people to do as he wished, and I'd always thought that included me, too.

Could it be true? That his powers had never worked on me? I'd repelled his efforts when he tried to make me open the door to my apartment, which felt like eons ago, but he'd implied it hadn't worked because he hadn't placed that much effort into it. Did this mean I was too strong for him to manipulate with magic?

I'd assumed the worst of Ryker, because the worst was easier to believe and what life usually dished out for me.

If his touch didn't control me magically, that meant I had to take responsibility for the way I felt about him.

Dammit!

I loved him and I wanted someone to blame.

Finally, the door hissed closed behind us and we were alone.

"I have something for you," Ryker said.

"If it's a dagger ready to stab me in the back, I'd rather you keep it to yourself," I said hotly.

"It's something I think you'll want." Heat blazed to life in his eyes as he reached behind and pulled—probably out of his ass—a crown.

I jerked back a step. "What are you doing?"

"Isn't it obvious?" He chuckled again. "I'm giving it to you."

"No." I shook my head. "This is some sort of trick. You want the throne. You want this crown."

His lips quirked up at the corners. "I have my own crown."

I stammered and blinked at him.

"Hell can have two rulers, Sloane. It hasn't for a long time, since demons don't typically know how to share." He held out the crown like a dare. "But I do."

What would happen if I refused? What would happen if I took the damn thing?

"Heavy is the head who wears the crown," I said under my breath. "Isn't that the saying? I'm not sure why you're giving it to me, Ryker."

"I refused to kill you during our trial." He dropped his gaze to his feet, although his hold on the crown remained steady. "You didn't know that. You were so dead-set on seeing me the way you wanted to see me that I never had a chance to explain. But I never planned to hurt you. I knew it would never come to that as soon as I realized the last trial would be Moloch's creation. Do you know what the last trial tested?"

"Death," I answered simply. "Murder? Betrayal?"

"Sacrifice. The last trial tested sacrifice, Sloane, and you demonstrated that by giving up the throne for me. I demonstrated it by letting go of my vendetta against your family and refusing to hurt you. We both won."

I squeezed my eyes shut and balled my hands into fists. "You bastard. You knew our lives were never in danger. If I had attacked you, you would've won."

He had the nerve to look sheepish, giving me a lopsided grin and a one-shouldered shrug. "In my defense, I knew you'd live even if you didn't win the throne. I knew the second you embraced your demon the disease destroying you would disappear."

My eyes pinged open and I screeched at him.

He smirked.

"Then...why? You could've told me earlier and I would've stepped aside. You could've had the throne all to yourself."

"That's exactly why I didn't."

After a moment of seething and resisting the urge to throttle him, I took a deep breath and asked, "So, what now?"

"We share the throne."

"There's got to be a trick," I repeated. The words sounded weak to me, and I didn't want to believe them.

He hadn't been poised to kill me with that sword. I thought back to the trial and ran through the events. Ryker had never attacked. I had thought he'd wanted me to initiate the fight so he could feel better about killing me.

Chupey had tried to tell me Ryker hadn't done what I thought, but like everything my familiar said lately, I ignored it.

Tears burned the sides of my eyes once again. Why was that always happening around him? He constantly caught me off guard, and it wasn't fair.

"What's not fair?" Ryker asked.

Oh. I must've said that last part out loud. "It's not fair that you affect me so much."

Understanding flashed in his gaze. "And you don't think you have the same effect on me?"

I waved at him, head to foot, trying to wordlessly point out his calm, composed demeanor, lack of shaking, and dry eyes.

Ryker chuckled and shook his head.

"It's not funny."

"It really is." He reached forward and snatched a strand of hair that had escaped my braid. Tucking the hair behind my ear, his expression softened. "I was a wreck after you left. I kept waiting for you to realize the last trial was a tie and return, but you didn't. I couldn't eat. I couldn't sleep. I couldn't accept the crown they kept shoving into my hands. I spent all this time pouring over ancient manuscripts to find evidence of dual rulers so I could present my interpretation of the last trial to the council. So I could demand they honor the tie. I've missed you so much."

"And you hate me for it."

"Always," Ryker said, without missing a beat. "I hate you so much sometimes. I hate what you do to me. And I hate that I love it."

"So that's mutual?"

He nodded. "Rule the Underworld with me, Sloane. It's your right, and I want you there beside me."

"You've really changed your tune since we first met," I said. "You were hell-bent on hating me and seeing your vendetta through. What happened?"

He dropped the arm holding the crown to his side. "*You* happened. You got in my mind and wormed your way into my heart."

He sounded pained.

"Ah, so I'm like a tapeworm."

"The sexiest tapeworm I've ever seen in my life." He didn't laugh at my joke. He waited, expression flashing between pained and serious.

"We're never going to work together," I told him. "You have to know that. Even if you want to share the throne, which I highly doubt, we wouldn't be good together. You'd want to kill me more times than not."

"Oh, every single day, I'm sure."

I balked. "You're not supposed to agree with me."

Ryker took another step toward me, until he stood so close his minty breath mingled with mine. I wanted to close my eyes and revel in him and what were surely lies. Except a large part of me desperately wanted to believe he wasn't lying. That he actually felt the same way for me as I felt for him and that all of this would work out.

Just fantasies, all around.

I needed something to do with my hands, so I gently took the crown from him, turning it over and over.

"You want to share this with me? Are you serious?"

"Deadly." His hands wrapped around mine to tighten my hold on the crown. "You belong in Hell, wearing this. And you belong with me. I'm not going to let you go again, Sloane. I meant it when I said you were mine."

"Oh, sure. You're going to physically haul me back to Hell and force my ass on that throne?"

I liked the imagery of it.

"If I have to." Ryker nodded. "I'm not leaving here without you. You don't belong in this cage, although I love the way you kick the shit out of everyone who tries to come up against you."

"And Chupey?"

"I wouldn't think of leaving him behind. Trust me."

"What about Zi'rel? She hates me."

"She hated the heartache you caused me. She'll come around."

Ryker lifted the crown, and my hands along with it, to the top of my head. He pried my fingers loose so that the crown perched, exactly where it was meant to be. Magic zinged through my blood, bonding with the crown and opening an awareness inside me. For a brief moment, I saw a face, my face but different. A man smiled at me, one that I recognized from the portrait in the castle's foyer, before it disappeared all together.

My father.

I gasped and squeezed my eyes shut, trying to chase the image down to see his face one more time, but he was gone.

"Come on," Ryker said. "We've wasted enough time."

"You really gave up your vendetta for me?"

"You're worth it."

He made it sound so simple.

I couldn't take it anymore and wrapped my arms around his neck, rising on tiptoe to place my lips on his. At once, everything clicked into place. Ryker, the throne, everything.

"You're sure you aren't making this happen?" I murmured against his lips.

Groaning, his arms banded around my waist to yank me closer. "Promise."

I lost myself in him. In his scent, his kisses, and the touch of his fingers skimming along my spine.

And I knew there was no place I'd rather be.

Well, except ruling Hell.

But we'd get to that soon enough.

EPILOGUE

I bounced on top of Ryker as he filled every inch of me, and I loved it. There was something about Hell that lowered the inhibitions and turned me into this siren, this creature, this queen.

And Ryker worshiped me for it.

His arms came around me and I squealed as he reversed our positions. Tossing me down onto my stomach and spreading my legs before spearing through me. His large hand came down in a hard whack on the side of my ass. I moaned at the contact.

He proceeded to spank the other side—symmetry, after all—and rode me until I lost the capacity for rational thought.

I didn't remember my own name by the time we were done but apparently Ryker did. After he came, moaning my name, he pulled out with a kiss to my cheek and one last spank for the road.

"Come on," he urged. "We've got to get going."

I rolled on my back with a groan, still feeling him written on my insides and enjoying the aftershocks of my own orgasm.

"We don't have to rush," I told him.

"Yes, we do."

He shot me a look over his shoulder that said I was being crazy.

"We're the monarchy. We're royalty. Things will start when we say they start." I wanted to bask in the afterglow, but despite my words, he had a point. We couldn't delay proceedings because I relished my orgasm.

If I pushed the matter, Ryker would support it though. He certainly never complained when I pounced on him, full of need. It was one of the things I loved most about him—the way he indulged me. I would've never expected that type of behavior from him when we first met. Love made fools of us all, didn't it? At least, it did with me.

I leaned up on my elbows to watch Ryker as he strode naked across our room to get dressed. Honestly, I could stare at that ass all day.

Eventually, I roused myself out of bed and met him across the room. He stole a searing kiss before pushing me toward the bathroom.

"Get cleaned up, my queen. We have an audience waiting."

Queen. He called me his queen. It was an upgrade from princess, for sure, and it was growing on me.

But as much as I didn't want to stop our fun, I knew he was right. The duties of the Underworld never ceased.

Less than twenty minutes later, I sat on the throne with Ryker by my side. His fingers laced through mine and the look on his face told me we'd pick up where we left off as soon as possible.

A throat cleared. I glanced to the left and Zane caught my gaze, a jerk of his head urging me to pay attention to the petitioners rather than my king.

I rolled my eyes at my friend. Zane could be such a stickler sometimes, but he was a great guard, and I knew better than to ignore his warnings at this point. The crown had become heavier since I first put it on, although I was lucky. I had people there to advise me, to guide me, and make sure I didn't mess up beyond repair.

It was the first time in anyone's working memory there had been two Lucifers on the throne, and although it took the court a bit of time to get used to it, one spearing look from Ryker had all naysayers falling silent.

Good.

I'd hate to kick their asses.

"Fucking uncomfortable," Ryker muttered, adjusting his seat and pointing down at the velvet beneath us.

I patted his cheek. "Maybe you're just getting old."

He scoffed. "Maybe you need to watch that mouth of yours."

Our gazes locked and an awareness snapped between us. Instantly, I knew exactly what he'd like to watch my mouth do.

My smile stretched from ear to ear and somehow, miraculously, we made it through the first round of petitioners without mishap. I might have almost swallowed my tongue a few times but the two of us managed. Even Zane looked relieved when he nodded, calling a pause to the proceedings.

"How many hours does this go on, again?" I asked him with a wince.

"All day," Zane answered, winking.

"All day? And we just have to sit here and listen?"

Chupey trotted up from where he'd been in the audience and sat at my side, his tongue lolling from the side of his mouth. "Could be worse."

"And it could be a lot better with a mimosa in my hand," I retorted.

The request was filled almost immediately by one of the demon underlings. Wow. This kind of service was something I could get used to. Easily.

Ryker was right about the throne being uncomfortable, though, I couldn't feel my left knee, and had pins and needles in my right ankle.

"We might have to invest in some new cushions or

something," I bent over to whisper. "Because I can't go all day."

"Who's old now?" Ryker replied, his chest rumbling with a deep chuckle.

"We're spoiled. That must be what it is. Our bed is so soft that nothing else can compare."

He lifted my free hand to his mouth and kissed the top of my knuckles. "Later, baby, later."

I finished off the mimosa in the next few minutes, listening to the growing crowd outside of the doors to the throne room. In mere moments, they'd swarm inside, asking questions and boons of the two of us and hoping for the best answer.

I might not always make the right choices, but I had to trust myself.

I slid my hand beneath my butt and massaged to get some of the feeling back. Until my fingers brushed the edges of something crumpled.

"What the..." I trailed off, dragging a black envelope out from underneath me and pinching it between my index and middle fingers. The envelope with the letter from my father. I recognized it immediately. I'd never opened it and when I returned to my apartment after the last trial, it had gone missing.

"You found something?" Ryker asked.

I shook my head, not trusting my voice.

When I finally opened the envelope and saw my name at the top, tears pricked my eyes and unaddressed emotions threatened to overwhelm me.

Sloane,

Just know, no matter what you've gone through to get to this point, I'm sorry. And I love you. Your life hasn't been easy with your bloodline, but I'm sure you've made the most of it, because you're too strong to do otherwise. You have the same fire as your mother.

In the upcoming weeks, you will learn things about who I am, what I've done, and what I became. It is my wish for you to take my place as Lucifer and right some of the wrongs of the past.

You'll make a great leader. I felt it in my bones the moment you entered this world, screaming.

I love you, daughter.

And I'll see you soon.

— DAD

I stared down at the paper until my eyes crossed. He'd...see me soon?

"What in the good fuck does that mean?" I asked out loud, shock coursing through my system. I wasn't shocked that a magical letter found me once I sat my cute little rear down on the throne. Magic was capable of truly great things. So that wasn't the surprise. His parting words were.

My father telling me he'd see me soon? Either that meant I was going to die...

Or my dear old dad was still alive.

CHARACTERS

Ba'al – demon of seduction and fertility

Becca – Sloane's best (and only) friend

Borca – Fomorian giant

Chupey – Chupacabra demonic familiar

Greg – Underground bookie

Gwyn – demon of the wild hunt

Ifrit – demon of the dead

Malachi – demon of trickery and traps

Mobius – demon competitor from Malachi's domain

Moloch – demon of sacrifice

Ryker Dante – tall, dark, brooding asshole...you know the type

Slade – Ryker's best friend

Sloane – Seriously, did you even read the book?

S'gor – demon of hatred and war

Wrathen – Demon mount

Zane – demon guard to the Immortal Throne

Zi'rel – Ryker's familiar

Siblings...they can be the death of you...

Raven Crawford knows better than to venture into the seductive world of the dark fae or agree to any of their salacious promises. She plans to pay off her debts so she can get on with her life and stay far away from the denizens of the Underworld.

Unfortunately, her numbskull twin steals from the most tempting and lethal fae of them all. Now, Raven must help the Lord of Shadows get back what her idiot brother stole. Her only weapons? Just a little ingenuity and a whole lot of snark. It's suicide for sure, but she'll do anything to protect her twin.

A darkly delicious Urban Fantasy tale with a flawed waitress trying to save her brother

by International Bestselling Author, J. C. McKenzie.

Buy *Conspiracy of Ravens* to start this series today!

Life's a b*tch--but what comes after isn't much better.

Jade Blackwell, a paranormal reaper, helps supernaturals cross over after death. Her job comes with lots of rules--but not following them is kind of her thing...until it ends up involving her in something much deadlier than she ever imagined.

With the protective veil fading away, demons are crossing realms and impregnating humans, and Jade's best friend is among their victims. She's determined to save her friend, even if it means working with Cole Masters, a dangerous demon halfling and notorious gun-for-hire.

But time is running out to fix the barrier and find a demon cure. With supernaturals everywhere in danger, and the balance between good and evil tipped for the worst, Jade must choose between her own eternal afterlife...or the living world she so desperately wants to be a part of.

Either way, death is coming.

The explosively popular Urban Fantasy genre meets a spunky new grim reaper tale by USA Today Bestselling Author, Harper A. Brooks.

Buy Death Wish to start the darkly unique series today!

ABOUT J. C. MCKENZIE

J. C. McKenzie is a book loving, gumboot-wearing, unapologetic science geek. She predominantly writes urban fantasy and post-apocalyptic dystopian fantasy with strong romantic elements. When she's not spinning tales, she's in the classroom sharing her passion for science and mathematics while secretly warping the young impressionable minds of our future to carry out her evil plans for world domination. She lives in the Pacific Northwest with her family.

Visit her at jcmckenzie.ca

- facebook.com/j.c.mckenzie.author
- twitter.com/JC_McKenzie
- instagram.com/j.c.mckenzie
- tiktok.com/@jcmckenzieo
- bookbub.com/authors/j-c-mckenzie

ABOUT HARPER A. BROOKS

Harper A. Brooks lives in a small town on the New Jersey shore. Even though classic authors have always filled her bookshelves, she finds her writing muse drawn to the dark, magical, and romantic. But when she isn't creating entire worlds with sexy shifters or legendary love stories, you can find her either with a good cup of coffee in hand or at home snuggling with her furry, four-legged son, Sammy.

RONE AWARD WINNER
USA TODAY BESTSELLING AUTHOR
INTERNATIONAL BESTSELLING AUTHOR

Join Harper's reader group for exclusive content, sneak-peeks, giveaways, and more!

facebook.com/harperabrooks

twitter.com/harperabrooks

instagram.com/harperabrooks

tiktok.com/@harperabrooks

ACKNOWLEDGMENTS

We'd like to thank Red Head Editing for the editing, Book Nook Nuts for the proofreading, Krista Cook for beta reading, and Natasha Art from Infinity Designs for the cover.

But most of all, we'd like to thank you, the reader. You're the best.